Stolen Dove

Dahlia Vale

Stolen Dove

Cover and Editing by CS Author Services

For the good girls who would dry hump their captor
for a fucking orgasm.

Note to Readers

Thank you so much for picking up my book! I'm so fucking glad you're here. But let's be clear about what you're getting yourself into.

I do not write slow burn or long novels. The stories are fast-paced, insta-heat, and the characters decide what they want and take it. The spice happens quick and often. And there is heavier smut to plot ratio. If you prefer a longer, slow-burn story, my world may not be for you, and that's OK! I still love you!

This is a dark romance and a work of fiction. I do not personally condone the actions, choices, or moral chaos of my characters. None of this should be taken as real-life advice or instruction. It exists purely for your *morally dark, alpha male, smut-loving pleasure.*

In this world, my characters don't use safe words, color systems, or any other form of structured kink communication. They're messy. They're unfiltered. They make terrible decisions and never apologize for them. This is not a guide to healthy kink dynamics—this is fantasy, and it's meant to be deliciously unhinged. (And my characters fucking love it!)

My entire world centers around a secret society of ruthless billionaires who play by their own rules. Expect power imbalance, manipulation, and twisted devotion.

So settle in. Expect explicit heat, an excessive use of F-bombs, questionable morals, and dark alpha-holes who are only redeemable to the women they ruin themselves for.

Welcome to *The Ravens.* Enjoy the fucking show.

Content Notice

I care about you all, so I have to cover this part. This is a DARK romance. These men are hot, but they are NOT heroes. That means it gets intense, messy, unhinged, morally black and all the things.

I do my best to note things and include them on my website to ensure a safe reading experience. If I miss something, it's not from lack of care. It's proof that I'm human, and don't always get it right. Drop me a note so I can update my website.

If you have any kind of content concerns, please check the detailed content warnings on my website before diving in. Just know that doing so may reveal spoilers. Consider yourself warned and please,

please, please keep yourself safe and check them if you have concerns: https://dahliavale.com/content-warnings/

Playlist

The official *Stolen Dove* playlist is available on Spotify!

"Closer" - Nine Inch Nails

"Skin" - Rihanna

"Earned It" - The Weeknd

"Villain" - K/DA, Madison Beer, Kim Petras

"You" - Regard, Troye Sivan, Tate McRae

"Wicked Game" - Chris Isaak

"Dangerous Woman" - Ariana Grande

"RUNAWAY" - half•alive

"Runnin' (Lose It All)" - Naughty Boy ft. Beyoncé

"Power & Control" - Marina

"Hands to Myself" - Selena Gomez

"Twisted" - MISSIO

"Control" - Halsey

"Obsessed" - Maggie Lindemann

"Mine" - Bazzi

"Love Me Like You Hate Me" - Rainsford

"Unholy" - Sam Smith, Kim Petras

"Often" - The Weeknd

"Slow Hands" - Niall Horan

"Bedroom Hymns" - Florence + The Machine

"Devil I Know" - Allie X

"I Found" - Amber Run

"BURY A FRIEND" - Billie Eilish

"In the End" - Tommee Profitt ft. Fleurie

"Warriors" - 2WEI, Edda Hayes

"Die For You" - The Weeknd

"Death of a Bachelor" - Panic! At The Disco

"Lost on You" - LP

The Ravens

Welcome to the Ravens! Here's your cheat sheet to the secret society that ties everything, and everyone, in my world together.

If you'd rather go in blind and let the way the society works reveal itself as you read...

Now's your chance to skip ahead.

.

.

.

Still here? You're about to learn the details about this ruthless secret society.

Ravens: Official male members of the society. Branded with a Raven on their wrist when they are twenty unless they have to serve as a Talon.

Doves: The women in the Ravens. Some serve as a Talon's Dove, and ALL are ultimately married off to a Raven.

Talons: Future Ravens who do the dirty work to earn their brand. They serve five years before they are branded as a Raven. The first four years they take an oath of celibacy other than one night a year during the annual ceremony when they fight to the death and surviving earns them a single fuck and another dick piercing right after. The last year they get to hunt in the woods for a Dove who is theirs to fuck for the year before their respective marriages are arranged by their parents (not usually to their Dove).

The Council: The governing body made up of the oldest living male heir from twenty founding families who control everything within the society.

Velum: Popular club where Ravens go to dance, drink, fuck, and do business without questions.

Graves U: University run by the Ravens with a mixture of Raven families and other elite families sending their children there.

Rules:

- Marriages are often arranged with the fathers doing most of the negotiations. The Council can override and make decisions about marriages.

- Marriages are sealed with public claimings. The man fucks the woman the way he wants in front of the Society to claim her as his. Talons must also publicly claim their Doves.

- Widows are auctioned if their fathers don't reclaim them... or if their late husbands' wills say otherwise.

- Families who have been Ravens for three generations or less must have their children serve: either as a Talon or a Talon's Dove. If the Talon fails, the family may be excommunicated or killed.

- Once you're in, you don't leave. Ever.
- The police don't interfere. The Talons handle punishment and enforcement. (And they are controlled by the Sinclairs)

Headquarters:

- Outside of Boston in New England, USA.

Established:

- Early 1800s

CHAPTER 1

BRIAR

The motel room smells of stale cigarettes and urine.

This is just perfect. This is what my life is now, and it's still an improvement.

Every sound from the parking lot keeps me on edge. Shadows passing by my window make me flinch. I hate how my body won't let me relax, even though I'm free.

Free? That's a joke. A Dove is never free.

But life on the run in a shit motel is far better than returning. Better than going back to be auctioned off by The Ravens to live a life at an aged asshole's mercy.

I count the cash for the third time in an hour, my fingers shaking so hard I drop some bills. Thirty thousand and four hundred dollars. Everything I could grab from Roland's safe before I made my escape.

The bills are dirty in my hands, like they carry the stench of him. Like cigars and expensive whiskey.

I've spent less than two hundred so far. Bus fare, this motel room, and underwear. In my frantic packing to escape after Roland's funeral, I failed to pack underwear, which is problematic when all I own is dresses.

I'm doing my best to lie low while I figure out my life. I only hope that the Ravens won't find me and drag me back to hell. That they will let me go.

Because if they want me back, I'm uncertain there is anywhere I could hide. The Ravens have unlimited resources and worldwide reach. They are a collection of families who've controlled New England for two centuries, with many others who have bought their way in. The women are raised to marry, have their children, and bend to their will.

The moment Roland's body was cold, my sentence should have been over. But in our world, they auction widows off if there isn't an agreement made in advance. They expect that I'll stand in front of hungry, aged widowers desperate for another chance to take on a beautiful, young wife.

And so I ran.

I catch my reflection in the mirror. I look like hell. Hair unwashed and pulled into a messy knot. My skin has a dirty tinge to it. And I'm wearing a fucking sundress.

"You can do this," I whisper to myself. But the woman in the mirror doesn't look convinced. But she will beat them. She has to.

The shower calls to me. It's been three days and I haven't been brave enough to let my guard down to shower, but it's time. I might even let myself go to a store soon to buy a pair of jeans. Another 'fuck you' to Roland.

I check the door lock. Then check it again before I wedge a chair under the handle for good measure.

I grab a clean pair of underwear and a different dress. Dresses. All dresses. Because that's all Roland let me wear. It's what he liked, so that's what I had to wear. Day in and day out...for over eight years.

The shower is barely functional, more rust than chrome, but the water is hot. And as soon as I step inside, it's heaven.

I let the warm streams soothe my body, relaxing for the first time since I ran. I make use of a razor to smooth my stubbled skin, and after I've finished, I chastise myself. No longer do I need to shave my legs for my bastard husband. He's dead.

But I can't deny that I prefer the softness.

I'm lathering my hair with shampoo when I hear the door creak. I jump back against the shower wall.

Soap is running into my eyes, making them burn, but I am frozen in place. My heart is racing so hard that the pounding is in my ears.

"Hello, Briar."

That voice makes me gasp, and I clasp my hand over my mouth to silence myself. I don't recognize it. The voice is male and deep. He's definitely a Talon sent to drag me back.

I look around the shower for something to defend myself with. The best I can hope for is blinding him with soap.

"I'm going to leave a towel on the counter." His voice is closer now, and I'm naked with only a thin curtain between us. "You're going to dry off, dress yourself, and we'll have a little chat about what happens next."

"Who are—"

"You know why I'm here."

He's a fucking Talon. I wonder which lesser Raven family he's a son of.

"I'll be in the room," he continues, his footsteps moving away from the shower. "You have five minutes. Don't make me come back in here."

The door clicks shut.

I stand there, water running over me, my brain screaming at what to do next. I could run...but where? The window is too small, and I have no chance of outrunning him. Fight? With what? My bare hands against a trained killer? And if I comply, then I end up back in Boston on an auction block.

I'm fucked no matter which way this goes.

I turn off the water with shaking hands and grab the towel.

Once I am dry, I pull on the underwear, and then the dress. I skip the dirty bra since I don't think I can manage the clasp with the shake in my hands. I stare at the bathroom door, trying to force my breathing to steady. This is fine. I'll talk to him and look for an opportunity to run. Maybe there's a way to negotiate. I have come this far, so I can't give up hope.

But who am I kidding? Talons don't negotiate.

When I open the bathroom door, I see him immediately. He's sitting on the corner of the bed. The chair that failed to secure the room is broken on the floor. He appears bored and unbothered by the situation. Like he isn't here to ruin my hope for a real life and drag me back into another horrible marriage.

I should look anywhere else because the more I stare at him, the more I struggle to breathe.

He's the most attractive, sexy man I've ever seen. And the way he's staring back at me has me frozen in place. The man is muscular, with dark wavy hair. Even sitting, I can tell that he's tall and would tower over me in his expensive jeans and tucked-in button-down shirt.

To top it off, the bastard has the sleeves rolled up so I can see the flex in his arms.

If I'd ever had a satisfying sexual experience in my life, maybe I wouldn't be practically salivating over the gorgeous man here to capture me.

His face is all sharp angles and full lips that likely never smile. He's attractive in a way that is almost vicious, like admiring a wolf right before it takes you down.

His piercing gray eyes lock onto mine. His broad shoulders strain against his shirt, and there's a scar cutting through his left eyebrow that somehow makes him more attractive instead of less, which pisses me off. Everything about him screams predator. The kind that doesn't need to rush to capture you, because he knows you're already caught.

And my body—my stupid, traitorous body—responds. I press my thighs together, trying to will the sensation away. The pressure is better than any touch my dead husband ever gave me.

He's studying me, too. Those gray eyes rake over me slowly and thoroughly. I'm not wearing a bra. My nipples are visible through the thin cotton—from cold, from fear, from the fucking arousal I can't control.

His gaze lingers on my chest. Only for a second. But long enough for me to know he noticed.

I see a twitch in his lips. At least he isn't unaffected.

"Sit." He gestures to the bed.

"I'd rather stand."

"That wasn't a request."

I sit at the opposite corner from him. The bed creaks, and I'm far too aware that I'm sitting on the same bed as this devil.

My mind races, and I remember he's here to drag me back. I look at other details besides his appearance. He has no visible weapons, but that doesn't mean he's unarmed.

"Roland's been dead for days," he says, like we're discussing the weather. "The widow auction will occur soon. You knew they wouldn't let you go. And they expect you to be compliant upon your return."

My stomach turns. Compliant. That is what Roland used to say before he struck me. That I need to learn to be a compliant Dove. The memory makes bile rise in my throat, but underneath the revulsion is nothing but rage. Pure, burning rage that my father had married me off to Roland to begin with. And that these Raven fuckers expected that I'd been beaten into submission enough to be a good investment for the men at auction.

Not that all marriages in our society are like mine, or even the ones formed at auction. But after all that I've survived. I refuse to go back.

"You've caused quite a stir by running," he continues. "Three men have placed sealed bids already."

"Good for them." The word comes out as more of a growl.

His lips twitch again. It's almost a smile. "I like that. Women with fire are so much more interesting."

"So you have someone to break?"

He leans closer, his fist pressing into the mattress between us. "Breaking's easy. Any idiot can break a person. It's something else entirely to know exactly how much pressure to apply before the person... yields."

The way he says that last word makes everything inside me clench. Because I understand what he means. Roland broke things—furniture, bones, spirits. He was all blunt force and rage. But I know the man before me is far more dangerous.

And my body likes it. My body is responding to the promise in his words, and I don't understand why. Roland touched me for eight years, and I had nothing but revulsion and pain. Not an ounce of pleasure that I heard was part of being intimate with a man.

He told me I was frigid. Broken. Normal women enjoyed their husbands, but I was too cold, too damaged, too horrible of a wife and a disgrace to all the Doves to respond the way my body should.

And he had cameras on me at all times, so I couldn't explore my body for myself.

So why am I reacting this way now? Why is blood rushing in my ears and my thighs pressing together and breathing becoming impossible? Why am I already imagining what it would be like to be touched by this man?

I'm sick. That's all there is to it.

"And now you are going to be a good girl while I take you back."

The panic returns, but I meet his eyes. "And who are you?"

"Does my name matter?"

"I'd like to know who's dragging me back to hell."

He considers me for a long moment, as if he's deciding whether I've earned a response. "Cain."

Cain. A biblical murderer. It's the perfect name for him. There's little doubt he's killed for Ravens, and he'll do it again. He'll do the job he's been trained for.

"This mission is about you, Briar Whitmore. And I assure you that I have done thorough research."

"You're twenty-eight. Married to Roland Whitmore at nineteen—"

"I know my own history."

He continues. "No children. No siblings. Your father is James Sutton of the billionaire textile family. Not a founding family but respectable Raven standing."

I huff and cross my arms. "You forgot my favorite color and childhood pet."

"Blue. And you never had pets. Your father didn't believe in them."

He acts like he's reading a grocery list instead of the details of my life.

His eyes never leave mine. "You broke three ribs when Roland threw you down the stairs two years ago."

My breath catches. No, he couldn't know.

"You told the doctor you fell, and you didn't report him because he threatened to kill your father if you did. You believed him because Roland was many things, but he wasn't a liar."

He knows. He knows about the worst day of my marriage, the day I realized Roland would kill me if he got angry enough. The day I had retreated into a shell of myself.

"But how..."

"It's my job to know everything about what I'm sent to retrieve. And tapping into Roland's security cameras wasn't all that difficult."

He actually used the word 'retrieve' like I'm a package. A thing. But the casual way he says it bothers me less than it should. Maybe because at least he's honest about what I am to him. Not a person. Not even really a problem. I'm an object that needs to be returned to its proper place. His mission.

"I'm not going back."

"Yes, you are. You are forever a Dove, and you belong to them."

"I'll die first."

I see him almost smile. The fucker is amused at my outburst.

"No, you won't. Want me to tell you how I know? Because people who are really ready to die don't run. They give up. You're not looking to die, Briar. You want to live. Which is exactly why you'll survive what comes next."

The words hit hard. He's right, and I fucking hate it. I want to argue, to tell him he's wrong, but we both know he isn't. I ran because I want to live. Really live, not just exist. And that desperate want is exactly what's going to get me dragged back.

"Surviving isn't living, Cain." I like the way his name sounds on my lips far too much.

"Better than being dead."

I laugh. I can't help it. The sound comes out wrong, jagged and bitter. "You don't get it. You can't possibly understand."

"I understand more than you think." His expression shifts for a second, then hardens again. "But it doesn't change the job."

"Everything is a choice."

"Is it?" He stands, and I watch him tower over me. He's six-four at least. "Was marrying Roland a choice? Were those broken ribs a choice?"

I flinch. I didn't choose any of it. My father arranged the marriage when I was nineteen against my will. We are raised to marry within our society, but not all fathers force the decision. Roland's violence was just what could happen when you are property of the wrong Raven.

"How long have you been watching me?"

"Long enough."

"That's not an answer."

"They called me the morning after you disappeared. I have a complete file on you." He moves to stand before me. "It took me less than a day to find you."

Less than a day. Well, good for him. I had three days of freedom, with this hot asshole stalking me.

I smell him now. Some expensive cologne over something metallic. Gunpowder, maybe. It's sexy as hell. And my body is far too aware of him. Great. My body decides that now is the time to wake up after eight years of nothing. Fantastic timing.

This doesn't make sense. This shouldn't be happening. Roland spent our entire marriage convincing me I was broken, that my inability to respond to him proved something was wrong with me. And I believed him. Spent years thinking I was defective.

But now this stranger is in my space, a threat to my entire future, and my body wakes up like it's been waiting for years for this moment. What does that say about me? That I need danger to find pleasure? That I'm so damaged I respond to fear and violence?

"So what now?" My voice cracks. "You drag me back? Throw me on that auction block? Watch them sell me to another man like Roland?"

"Now we drive back to Boston. You attend the auction. Then you comply, and you survive."

"Survive." I want to spit at him. "You mean disappear. You mean die slowly, just like I did for the past eight years."

"I have a job to do." He appears unmoved.

"And you always do your job?"

"Always."

I stand to face the man who is almost a whole foot taller than me. But I cannot hold back my fury. The fear is still there, but my anger burns far hotter. "Must be nice. Being the Ravens' weapon. Following orders. Never having to think or feel or—"

Before I know what's happening, his hand wraps around my throat. Not squeezing hard, just holding me there. And I don't make an attempt to get away from him as I let him walk me backward across the room until I'm pinned against the wall.

I should fight. Should claw at him. Should scream until someone hears, even if it's just the meth addicts next door who wouldn't care anyway. But I can't move. Can't think past the weight of his palm against my windpipe, the way his thumb rests against my racing pulse.

This should remind me of Roland. I should start to choke and panic. But I don't. For some fucked up reason, I like being under his control. And a sick, twisted part of me I didn't know existed is responding to it. Somehow my body is coming alive in a way it hasn't before, and I don't want it to end.

"Careful." He warns.

His eyes drop to where his hand circles my throat, watching my reaction. A smirk forms on his lips, and god he's even more gorgeous.

Then his gaze meets mine again, and something flickers in his eyes.

He braces himself against the wall with his other hand, and his body presses against mine.

His closeness makes me whimper. I fucking whimper before I can stop myself.

I glance up to meet his stare, and his eyes darken slightly, pupils dilating. "You're wet for me, aren't you?"

"I...I..." I start to speak, but the words die when his grip tightens as if he expected me to lie.

I can't tell him the truth. He's right, and admitting it is the same as handing him a weapon. Like giving him ammunition to use against me later when I'm trying to maintain whatever scraps of dignity I have left.

He leans down, and his lips brush my ear when he whispers into it. "That's sweet, little Dove. But I'm still taking you back."

"You're full of yourself." Not a lie, but also not giving him the satisfaction of admitting the truth.

"Am I?" His lips brush across the top of my ear. "I could slip my hand beneath this thin little dress and see for myself."

God, I want him to do that. I want him to touch me. To prove that something beyond arousal is possible, that his touch would be pleasurable. That Roland was a broken fucker, not me. And that I can have a fucking orgasm.

The thought terrifies me almost as much as going back. That I'm so damaged and fucked up that my captor is turning me on.

"I hate you," I whisper.

"Maybe." His hand doesn't move from my throat. "But your body doesn't. Your body is very honest, Briar. Much more honest than you want to be."

He's right. I'm craving his control, and I want to know what would happen if I touched myself right in front of him.

But I can't give him that satisfaction. I can't give him more power to manipulate me or to make my body betray itself. If I allow him to, he'll dismantle me piece by piece, and deliver me back to auction as nothing but a puddle.

"Let me go." I don't sound like I mean it, but I have to say it.

His thumb presses harder into my throat. He's not cutting off air. He's reminding me he could if he wanted to. Reminding me who is in control.

And then he releases me and steps back, and I immediately miss his touch. My legs are shaking. And I hate myself for wanting more of him.

He watches me try to collect myself, and there's something in his expression now. Satisfaction, maybe. Or curiosity. Like I'm a puzzle he's just figured out how to solve.

"Pack your things. We leave in ten minutes."

The reality of the situation comes crashing back down on me. "You'll have to drag me out of here, Cain. Kicking and screaming. I won't make this easy for you."

"I didn't expect you to." He checks his watch. It's expensive and platinum. "And Briar? I don't mind if you fight. But the result will be the same."

I shiver at his words and feel the heat between my thighs. My resistance makes this better for him, and my fighting will only make whatever game he's playing more satisfying when he wins.

And we both know he'll win.

"Nine minutes now," he says.

I don't move. Can't move. I'm frozen between conflicting impulses. I could run and make him chase me, or even fight him to get his hands on my body again.

What is wrong with me that these are my thoughts?

"Briar." My name on his lips sounds different from when Roland said it. Darker and sexier in the best ways. Even if I'm imagining it. "I can do this two ways. You can pack your things, walk out calmly, and you get to sit in the front seat of my car. Or I can zip-tie your wrists, carry you out, and throw you in the trunk." He pauses. "Your choice."

I release a long huff and then grab my bag and start throwing things in. All of my fucking dresses. The cash goes in too, shoved into the bottom along with everything else. I hate him for making me give in so quickly. But I hate myself more that my body still wants him to touch me.

He takes the bag for me after I zip it closed, and the gesture is almost absurd given the situation. He's my fucking captor, not some gentleman carting my luggage around.

He walks to the door and opens it for me, and nods toward the black SUV parked right in front.

I look at it and then back at him, holding my bag. "I could run."

"You won't."

"How can you be so sure?"

He leans in close. So close I can see flecks of silver in those gray eyes. "Because I will never stop hunting you."

The certainty in his voice terrifies me most. It's not arrogance. Just a fact.

He guides me to the passenger door and opens it. He stands there until I'm settled in the black leather seat, and then he closes my door.

Cain tosses my bag into the back and then slides into the driver's seat.

"Buckle up, good girl."

Fuck, why do those words make me want to straddle him there in the SUV? But I push that thought aside and do as I'm told.

As we pull away from the motel, I stare into the side mirror. I have at most a few days left to enjoy my freedom, and I'm going to hope that they go by slowly. Even if it means being trapped in a car with Cain.

Once we get on the highway, the desert stretches ahead of us. There are two thousand miles between us and Boston. Days of driving before I am sold like I'm Roland's furniture at his estate sale.

I sneak a glance at Cain, and his jaw is tense.

Then his phone rings. He glances at the screen, and he groans before he answers it.

"I have her." A pause. His eyes cut to me briefly, then back to the road. "Two days, maybe three depending on the weather."

Another pause. Longer this time. His jaw tightens.

"That's not what we agreed." His voice drops and turns dangerous. "I'll have her back for the auction. You said—"

He stops to listen, and his knuckles go white on the steering wheel.

"Understood. I'll wait for confirmation."

He ends the call and tosses the phone into the cupholder with more force than necessary.

"Is something wrong?" I ask, hating how small my voice sounds.

"No."

But everything about his body language screams the opposite. The muscle ticks in his jaw. The way he won't look at me. The tension radiates from him.

"What did they say?"

He's quiet for a long moment. "Just a small change in plans."

My stomach drops. "What kind of change?"

"Just overnight locations. Nothing for you to worry about." He still won't look at me. "We will continue to Boston."

"Why does it matter where we sleep?"

"I follow orders. And right now, my orders are to stop where they say and to deliver you to the auction."

Right now? Who knows what else these sick fucks might have in store for me after I bruised their egos by running away from them.

"That's what this is really about, isn't it?" I press. "It's not about me. It's about making sure every other Raven woman knows what happens when you run. That the Ravens' reach is absolute. There's no point in trying."

"I see you finally understand your situation."

At least he's not pretending otherwise. At least he's not dressing it up as concern for my wellbeing or some bullshit about me being better off back in Boston.

"So I'm just a message."

"You're an example." He glances at me, and I can't read his expression. "Proof that running doesn't work. The Ravens will always win."

"The Ravens." I laugh, sharp and ugly. "And you are their Talon soldier who will kiss the ring to ensure you get your place within the council."

"We all play our part. And my job is to get you back before the auction. What happens after that isn't my concern."

He says it as if he's trying to convince himself. Like the words taste wrong in his mouth, but he's forcing them out. But I'm imagining it. He doesn't give a fuck what happens to me. That's nothing but wishful thinking.

Was that hope that had me practically panting when he had his hand on my throat? The ache hasn't gone anywhere. If anything, it's worse. And a constant reminder that my body's a traitor.

I had been minutes away from fucking him. When I've never even found fucking all that enjoyable. And I should call myself a crazy whore for being this way. But my entire life is batshit crazy.

I'm going back to put on an auction block because of centuries-old traditions that aren't even legal in this country. And they know I won't involve the police. The police can't help me.

So what difference would it make if I let the man beside me between my legs? I let Roland there, and he was the worst man I'd ever met in my life.

And a night with Cain is far more preferable to being auctioned to some sixty-year-old asshole who will blame me when he can't get it up.

No matter what happens on this pathetic excuse for a road trip, I'm fucked.

CHAPTER 2

CAIN

She hasn't said a word in three hours.

Briar sits there, pressed against the passenger door like she can phase through it if she tries hard enough. She's staring out the window at the endless desert finally turning to mountains.

She thinks I can't read her. She's wrong.

I watch the way she bites at her bottom lip, how her eyes dart while she plots what would be a failed escape, the subtle shift of her thighs as she fights the reaction she had to me.

And, fuck, I'm still hard from toying with her.

That sundress isn't helping matters. The black cotton hugs her in the right places. Her hard nipples are visible through the thin fabric, and I can't stop imagining how gorgeous her breasts would look bouncing as I fuck her. The hem hits just above her knee and rides up slightly every time she shifts position. And I can't deny I'm disappointed it hasn't ridden up enough for me to see if she has panties on under there.

If she does, I'm certain they're soaked.

I almost smile at it, but I'm suffering too much from the restraint of my jeans.

She's beautiful. There's no denying that. And she doesn't need hours of makeup and shit. Her blonde hair has dried into loose waves after her shower, and it makes me want to fist my hands in it while her mouth bobs on my cock. There would be nothing better than her watery eyes looking up at me as she gagged on my size.

Goddamn it. What a fucking waste that she was married to that shitstain husband.

But it doesn't matter what I think. She's my mission, and after I complete it, she's someone else's problem. She's a widowed Dove, and her place in the Ravens is to go to auction and take another husband.

I've done this job before. I can't say I enjoy doing it, but I'm good at tracking down the runaway Doves. And I must earn my place. At least that is what my father continues to remind me as he uses my talents to build relationships with the founders.

I wish I didn't want to fuck this one as badly as I do. That's never happened before, but there's something about Briar Whitmore.

I won't fuck her, but it makes the days of driving with her far more torturous. The sooner I get her to Boston, the better. I should have opted to put her in the trunk.

But I suppose this is entertaining.

She's hyperaware of me, pretending she's not but failing. I can see it in the way she holds herself too still, the way her breathing stays carefully shallow like deeper breaths might draw my attention. She hasn't looked directly at me since we got in the car, but I catch her watching my hands on the wheel in her peripheral vision.

This wasn't supposed to be complicated. Retrieve the runaway Dove. Deliver her to Boston. Nothing more and nothing less. It's what I do.

I adjust my grip on the steering wheel, forcing myself to focus on the road instead of the memory of her pulse racing beneath my hand. Every frantic beat pounded against my thumb. Her pupils dilated when I tightened my hold. Her lips parted right before her breathing changed. She didn't pull away.

Which means either she's an exceptional actress, or it turned her on.

I'm betting on the latter, which is why I can't get my cock to settle.

My phone buzzes. I glance at the screen. It's Garrett, my contact when I am out on missions.

"What do they want now?"

Briar's first words since we left Nevada.

I just shrug. Let her wonder. The text is simple enough.

The cabin coordinates are attached. Ensure she returns by any means necessary.

They don't care if I beat the hell out of her, as long as she is returned. They will make an example out of her, and based on the bids she's received, she won't have many freedoms.

It doesn't sit right with me. She's far too beautiful to be hidden away or to be marked by one of the pompous bastards. If I marked her... I'd make her enjoy it. I'm no hero, and her fate doesn't factor into the assignment. I never gave a fuck what happened to the others.

But bringing her back to the Ravens irritates me much more than it should.

"Why do you seem annoyed?"

"We're stopping soon," I tell her. That's all she needs to know.

"Where?"

"Somewhere secure."

She crosses her arms, and her breasts push up over the neckline of her sundress. "Somewhere I can't escape from."

I don't respond. We both know it's true.

She goes quiet again, but I catch the way her hands clench in her lap. I can see the way her mind races and the fight she has in her. Still looking for exits that don't exist, an escape that is not possible.

I respect that she hasn't given up. But I won't allow her to escape, no matter how hard she tries.

After a series of back roads, the cabin finally comes into view as the sun sets. It's isolated and surrounded by a dense pine forest with nothing else for miles in any direction.

I park and turn off the ignition. She doesn't move, just stares out the windshield at the cabin. Then, her gaze shifts to the trees surrounding us. Nothing but trees in every direction, and the nearest house isn't for miles.

I watch her throat work as she swallows. She's realizing just how alone we are. How far she'd have to run to find help. How no one would hear her scream.

Good. Let that sink in.

"Out," I command.

She opens the door and steps out of the SUV. It's a small victory that she won't make me toss her over my shoulder and carry her in.

I hope she tries to run—not because I wouldn't catch her. Damn right I would. But chasing her down and fucking her against a tree sounds far too tempting right now, and that's not part of the job.

I grab her bag from the back and move in behind her, urging her toward the cabin. Once we reach the door, I enter the code that Garrett gave me and the door unlocks. Then, I urge her inside and close the door behind us. It requires a code to open from the inside, too, which will keep her from attempting an overnight escape.

We move through the cabin, and I let her look around.

It's furnished and well-stocked for use when the Ravens require it. The main room is open with a couch and fireplace and a kitchen. There is one bedroom and one bathroom.

"There's only one bed," she says.

"Aren't you an observant one?" Even though I am absolutely an asshole, I don't intend to treat her like shit. But spending the night with her here is already making my cock hurt, and it's not even dark yet.

"Where am I supposed to sleep?"

"The bed." I drop her bag near the door. "I'll take the couch."

She blinks. She's surprised that I'd let her have the bed. Or that I wouldn't force myself on her.

She expected me to demand we share. That I would be like Roland—taking what I wanted because I could.

I'm a murderer and enforcer for The Ravens, but I don't fuck women who don't want it. That's the line, and when I pleasure a woman, it's because she begs for it.

"There's food," I say, ignoring her reaction as I turn away and move toward the small kitchen. "You should eat."

"I'm not hungry."

"Eat anyway." Her defiance was hot at first, but it's going to grate on my nerves if I have to force her to eat.

"Stop telling me what to do."

I turn to face her fully. She's standing in the middle of the room, arms crossed, chin lifted. There's color in her cheeks and fire in her eyes, and it does things to me I shouldn't be feeling.

There she is. The woman I glimpsed in that motel room is doing things to me that are inconvenient at best.

"I can make you, if you prefer." I move closer, watching her hold her ground even as her breathing picks up. "We can do it the hard way. But we both know how this ends."

Her jaw tightens. "I hate you."

"You've mentioned that."

She glares at me for another moment, then moves past me to the kitchen. She grabs an apple from the counter and takes an aggressive bite.

I call it a victory on my part. She's complying but making damn sure I know she doesn't like it.

I respect that more than I should.

I pour whiskey from the cabinet and offer her the bottle. Her eyes widen for a moment, and she just shakes her head.

Interesting. "Did Roland allow you to drink?"

She shakes her head as she finishes chewing another bite of her apple. "Roland didn't let me do a lot of things."

"Like wearing pants?" I nod toward her bare legs.

Her eyes snap to mine, and then she sets down the half-eaten apple. "Why do you care?"

"I don't." A lie. I find her intriguing as fuck.

"Then why bring it up?"

The more I learn about how he treated her—the control, the violence, the dimming of her passion—the more I wish I could have killed the bastard myself. And I can't tell her that. Because it's insane. I hardly know her, and I'm handing her back over to the Ravens in a few days.

"Professional curiosity."

She rolls her eyes. "Well, unless you have a pair of jeans I might fit, there's nothing else for us to discuss."

"That will make our days together much longer." I take a drink, welcoming the burn. "But I don't suppose you care if my job is simple."

"Your job." She laughs bitterly. "At least you're honest about it."

"Would you prefer I pretend this is something different?" I already do that.

"I'd prefer you let me go."

I laugh. "Not happening, little Dove."

"Why?" She moves closer, and I can smell the motel soap on her skin. "What makes you so loyal to them? What makes dragging a woman back to hell worth whatever they're rewarding you with?"

"I'm a Talon. This is what I do." At least that is what they drilled into our heads during initiation.

"That's not an answer."

"It's the only one you're getting."

She's close now, almost touching me. Close enough that I can see the green and gold in her eyes.

"You want to know what I think?" Her voice drops lower. "I don't believe you like this job as much as you pretend."

She's trying to find leverage by looking for any weakness she can exploit. It's actually a decent strategy. If I had any weaknesses, which I don't.

"Careful, Briar."

"Or what? You'll drag me back to Boston? Oh, wait—you're already doing that." Her hands fist at her sides, and her little tantrum is so damn cute. "What exactly do I have to lose by saying whatever the fuck I want?"

"I can make this trip very uncomfortable for you."

"You mean more uncomfortable than being kidnapped and dragged back to be sold?"

"I can always tie you up." And that idea does little to ease the mostly hard state I've been in since she walked out of that motel bathroom with wet hair and her black sundress.

Something shifts in her expression. A bit of fear maybe, but I would wager it's mostly desire. If I pinned her against the wall right now, I believe she'd be tempted to spread her legs for me.

My phone buzzes in my pocket. I pull it out, glancing at the notification. Another text from Garrett.

The second my eyes drop to the screen, Briar moves.

She lunges for the phone in my hand.

I catch her wrist easily, but she's already twisted, using my grip as leverage to throw herself off balance. We collide, and she stumbles forward, falling against me so I land on the couch behind me.

I catch her on the fall, my hands on her hips to steady her. She catches herself with palms flat on my chest, straddling me with her pussy pressed against my now fully hard cock.

For a second, neither of us moves.

Her weight settles against me, and her pussy is warm through my jeans. We haven't even done anything, and, fuck, she feels good.

She's flushed, breathing hard from the sudden movement, her eyes wide and uncertain. The thin cotton of her dress has bunched around her thighs.

I expect her to scramble off my lap. But she still isn't moving.

I should set her aside. Should lift her off of me and finish the job I set out to do and not make this complicated.

But I want to see what she'll do. And I never claimed to be a nice guy.

"Comfortable?" I ask, deciding that teasing her is the best path forward.

Briar blinks. She seems to just realize the position she's in. She shifts to move, and the rub of her pussy against me creates friction through my jeans that makes my cock throb.

Her breath catches. And then she moves again. Less accidental this time, grinding herself against me.

Interesting.

I'm not certain whether she thinks she has a chance of manipulating me or of using me. Either way, I'm not inclined to stop her. Not yet. Not when I want to see how far she'll take this.

If her goal is manipulation, I'll let her think it's working. Let her believe she has control when she doesn't. And when I still deliver her to Boston, she'll understand exactly how powerless she really is.

If she wants to use me for a bit of sex before she faces her future... well. That's more interesting.

She does it again. A slow roll of her hips. Her eyes have gone dark, lips parted, and she's watching my face like she's trying to read my reaction.

I tighten my grip on her bare thighs as her dress rides up. "Is this your play?" I practically growl. "You think if you fuck me, I'll let you go?"

She shakes her head, but her hips keep moving.

"Then what are you doing, Briar?"

"I don't—" She stops. Tries to speak again as she's dry humping me. "I don't know."

The honesty in those three words does something to me, but I ignore it. It must have been a long time since she's gotten off. Which is a damn shame. That aged husband of hers probably couldn't get it up.

I flex my hips up slightly to meet her next movement, increasing the pressure. Her eyes go wide, and her grip on my shoulders tightens.

"I can't—" The word comes out breathy. And I fight the urge to kiss her.

"Can't what?" I guide her hips into a slow rhythm. "Can't admit that even though you hate me, your body doesn't care? That your pussy is wet for me."

She's breathing harder now as she moves against my cock, and the little sounds she makes tell me she's about to come.

This is the hottest thing I've ever fucking seen. Her tits are bouncing as she rubs her pussy on me, and I can tell she wants to come more than anything.

Her movements turn frantic. She's chasing it, desperate and hungry for it. And fuck if I'm going to let her take it herself.

My hands lock down on her hips, stopping her from moving.

She whimpers and tries to move against my grip. "I was—please, I almost—"

"I know exactly what you want, little dove. But you forget who your captor is." I hold her still, watching her face flush and her full lips form an unsatisfied pout. "If you're going to come, it's because I let you."

"Please—"

"Please what?" I grind her down once, hard against my cock. "Say it. Beg me for it."

"I don't—I can't—"

"I guess you don't want it badly enough."

I'm an asshole, I know it. I don't give a shit. She's so sexy and responsive, and I want to drag out the moment as long as I can.

"Please, Cain, I need it. Please."

My dick is throbbing as she begs. I guide her hips again, moving her in a smooth rhythm. "Good girl. Isn't it better when I give it to you?"

She nods, and her head falls back. I can tell she's close. I want to stop again and torture her over and over. But I'm going to finish in my fucking jeans if I let her keep going like this, and if I allow myself to come, it's going to be inside of her.

"That's it. Now come for me, little dove."

I know the moment her body loses control. She shakes and moans. The sound she makes goes straight to my cock—half scream, half sob. She's trembling, nails biting into my shoulders.

Fuck, she's gorgeous. I'll never be able to get that image out of my head as long as I live.

Then the sobs take over. Her shoulders slump, and she covers her face with her hands.

"Briar?" I pull her hands away. "Look at me."

She shakes her head, sobbing harder.

After a few moments, her wet eyes meet mine, confused and ashamed.

"What happened?" I know I'm an asshole, but I didn't think she would regret it that much.

"I don't know. That's never—I've never—"

Oh fuck. Jesus fucking Christ. Eight years and that bastard never once made her come.

"You've never had an orgasm?"

She shakes her head. "He said I was broken." The words tumble out between sobs. "That something was wrong with me. That I was frigid and—"

If the fucker were still alive, I'd kill him. The least a man can do is give a woman a fucking orgasm. That isn't asking all that much.

She pulls away and refuses to look at me.

I let her stand in front of me as the skirt of her dress falls back in place. She wraps her arms around herself.

"I should—" She gestures toward the bedroom.

"Briar."

"Don't, please. I need a minute."

She runs. The door closes with a quiet click.

I sit there staring at the door in disbelief at what happened. Damn it, I'm still fucking hard. I want to beat the piss out of a dead man. I want to fuck. And I want to go after her and make sure she's alright. I never give a shit if anyone is alright, so I don't know why I care about Briar Whitmore.

Even still, I don't move.

In a few days, some rich asshole will buy her at auction. He'll take her home and use her the same way Roland did.

The thought almost makes me put my fist through the wall. It makes me want to toss her into the car and drive her somewhere the Ravens will never find her.

I'm a rich asshole, too. And now I fucking want her.

I pour another whiskey and hear the shower turn on from inside the bedroom.

I could keep her for myself. Take us both away from the Ravens. But it's not that simple. I have a job to do, and I don't get to choose a different path.

I have no choice but to take her back. But that doesn't mean I won't kill anyone who bids on her.

CHAPTER 3

BRIAR

I can't stop thinking about last night.

But not in a dreamy, romantic way. More like poking at a sore tooth—you know it'll hurt but you can't stop. Except instead of a tooth, it's the memory of me grinding on my captor's lap until I came so hard I cried.

So that's where my brain is at today.

I tried to recreate it this morning. I locked myself in the bathroom, turned on the shower for noise, and touched myself thinking about him. My fingers couldn't find the right rhythm. Even when all I could think about was his hands on my hips, guiding me against him, it still wasn't enough.

Roland spent eight years convincing me I was broken. Turns out I just needed to rub against my captor's cock. Apparently, it wouldn't have been all that difficult for my dead husband to get me off if he had given a shit. Congratulations to me for figuring that out right before they auction me off to another man who won't know where the clitoris is.

Perfect timing, universe.

Now I'm stuck in this car with Cain, and I can't look at him. I can't even glance in his direction without remembering exactly how pathetic I sounded when I begged.

We have been driving for hours, and he hasn't said a word to me. The prolonged silence is worse than my embarrassment. These are my last days of freedom, and this could be worse than facing the auction.

I release a loud huff at my dramatic thoughts.

"You could have just asked me to shower with you this morning," he responds.

My entire body goes rigid. "How—"

"I know everything."

My face heats. "You're a dick."

"You seem to consider it one of my best qualities." He glances at me with his smirk. "Did you get yourself off?"

"I thought you knew everything."

"I know you didn't, little dove."

I hate that he can read me so easily. And I especially hate that he knows exactly what I did and couldn't do. "Maybe I'm stressed, given you've fucking kidnapped me and are keeping me against my will."

"Maybe." He drums his fingers on the steering wheel. "But given the way your thighs are pressed together, I don't think you're all that eager to get away from me."

I force my legs apart just to prove him wrong, but the movement only makes me more aware of the ache between them. "You're imagining things."

His eyes drop to my thighs. "That's not helping your case."

I close them again and stare at his muscular forearms because apparently I'm a masochist now.

"I'm willing to bet that your pussy is soaked right now."

God, I hate him. And he's fucking right. Which makes me hate him more.

"Fine," I snap. "You win. I couldn't get myself off this morning. Happy? Want to add it to your report for the Ravens? 'Widow Dove unable to achieve orgasm without captor's help.' There."

He actually laughs—not an almost-smile or a smirk. An actual laugh that doesn't make him appear any less dangerous or sexy.

"I think we can omit that part. To spare you any further embarrassment."

"My hero. Just the important stuff then? Fugitive retrieved, delivered to auction block, buyers satisfied?"

"Something like that."

His jaw tightens, which is interesting.

"Why?" The question comes out before I can stop it.

"Why, what?"

"Why did you let me... why didn't you stop me?"

He considers this for a moment. "Did you want me to stop you?"

"That's not an answer."

"Neither was yours."

We drive in silence for a few miles. The tension doesn't dissipate. It builds with every mile, every breath, every time his hand moves on the steering wheel, and I imagine it between my legs.

"Eight years," he finally says. "That's a long time to spread your legs and get nothing for it."

"Don't." I don't want his pity. I don't want him psychoanalyzing my fucked up marriage.

His expression is unreadable. "When you were in that shower this morning, trying to make yourself come, what were you thinking about?"

"Stop."

"Did you want to know what it would feel like to be fucked by me?"

My breath catches, but I force myself to meet his eyes before he focuses back on the road. "Would it matter if I did, Cain?"

"You aren't asking the questions here, little dove. But I'll take that as a yes."

He's maddening. "So what? It felt good, and why shouldn't I enjoy what feels good while I still can?"

I glance between his legs and can see that he's hard. Good—I hope it hurts.

"I could definitely do that for you."

"I'm sure that's what you say to all the girls as you drag them back to hell."

He glances at me again. "Never."

I swallow hard, and the silence hangs between us for several moments. His admission makes my heart race faster.

"Now who's the liar?"

"I'm a lot of things, Briar. But a liar isn't one of them. Now are you going to answer my question?"

I can hardly think. Or breathe, for that matter. "What question?"

"What were you thinking about in the shower?"

"You know what I was thinking about."

"I want to hear you say it."

"Why? So you can feed your fucking ego?"

Fuck, he's going to drive me insane.

"Because I fucking said so."

I hate that I'm dripping now. My body is betraying me every second of this drive. "Fine. You want to know? I was thinking about your hands. Happy?"

"Where?"

"What?"

"Where were you thinking about my hands?"

Jesus Christ. He's really going to make me say it. "Between my legs. Obviously."

"Doing what?"

I glare at him, but he just raises an eyebrow. He acts as if we're discussing the weather instead of my pathetic shower fantasies.

"Your fingers were inside me," I say, the words coming out in a rush. "About how it would feel if you actually touched me instead of just letting me rub against you."

His jaw clenches. "And?"

"And what?"

"Was that all you were thinking about?"

"No." The admission burns coming out. "I thought about your mouth too."

"Where?"

"You know where."

"Say it."

"On my pussy. There. Are you happy? I was imagining you going down on me because Roland never did, not once in eight years, and I wanted to know what it felt like." The words tumble out, and I push aside how I feel like a desperate loser. "I wanted to know if it would feel better than grinding on you."

He's quiet for a moment, and I can't read his expression. Then he says, "I would make it feel much better."

My entire body is on fire, but I'll be damned if I let him know that. "You are certainly confident."

"I'd tie you up first. Wrists to the headboard. Maybe your ankles, too, spread wide so you couldn't close your legs."

Goddamn it. I rub my thighs together, wishing it would give me some kind of friction. Because he's making me need it.

"I'd make you earn each orgasm." His fingers drum on the wheel. "I'd edge you repeatedly until you're exhausted and begging."

And I want the fucking torture.

That's the problem, isn't it? There is no reason I should want Cain. He's attractive and his body feels far too perfect against mine.

But in every other way? He's wrong. So completely wrong. He's dragging me to an auction. He's my captor. And he's going to toy with me and then hand me over without a second thought.

And my body doesn't give a fuck.

One orgasm. That's all it took to turn me into this.

The wetness of my slit is becoming a problem. I shift again, but it doesn't help.

Nothing helps. That's what I learned this morning in the shower. My fingers don't work as well. Which means I'm stuck wanting something I can't give myself, from someone I shouldn't want it from.

One orgasm and my body woke up after eight years of sleep. Great timing.

We turn onto a two-lane road. That means we must be close to whatever remote cabin he's going to keep me captive in tonight.

I don't know how I'm going to survive another night with him.

I glance at him again and realize he's stopped teasing me. Instead, he's focused on watching the rear-view mirror.

"Cain, is something wrong?"

"Nothing for you to be concerned about."

I keep watching the car in the side mirror, wondering why Cain is so fixated on the car. We slow to make a right turn onto another small road, and the black car behind us speeds away.

Cain continues to check the mirrors and watch as he drives us down a few more back roads until we reach another cabin. It looks a lot like the first one did. It's small and remote.

He parks and turns off the engine. We sit in silence for a moment. I wish he'd just pull me into his lap and fuck me here in the car.

"Inside," he finally says. I fling open my car door in frustration as he grabs the bags.

I follow him to the door, watching him enter another code. The cabin layout is almost identical to the last. It has a small kitchen, living area, and one bedroom visible through an open door.

One bed again—because the universe fucking hates me.

He drops our bags near the entrance and moves into the main room to check the windows.

Once he's done, he faces me again. "You're tense."

"Gee, I wonder why."

"All that attitude." He leans against the doorframe to the kitchen, crossing his arms in front of him. I think he knows what his forearms do to me. "It's cute."

I roll my eyes at him.

His mouth quirks. "You could try telling me what you want. You seemed to enjoy that game."

Something very wrong inside me snaps. I'm done caring about what anyone else expects me to be. If I want him, I'm going to have him.

This is insane. He's taking me to be sold. And I'm about to beg him to fuck me.

I'm already going to hell. Might as well enjoy the ride.

"Fine." I move closer to him. "You want me to beg you? Then pretty fucking please, will you fuck me, Cain?" I bat my eyelashes at him with false sweetness.

His eyes go wide. He didn't expect me to actually say it. Good.

I slink even closer and don't give him a chance to respond. "If you're going to drag me back to that auction, don't I deserve one good fuck before some asshole decides he owns me?" My voice cracks, but I keep going. "So have pity on the needy widow, and fuck me already."

He stares at me for a couple of seconds, and I can't tell what he's thinking.

Then he moves fast, backing me against the wall.

"You think I'd fuck you out of pity?" His voice is low, and his hand wraps around my throat. "I don't do charity, Briar. I'm not moved by some pretty speech."

His thumb strokes my pulse point. "If I fuck you, it's because I want to. Because you're mine to use until I hand you over."

His words make me wetter.

I'm such a slut. Not that I've had enough experience to earn the title.

"But you're right about one thing." He brings his lips close to my ear. "You're going on that auction block. Some bastard is going to buy you. And you'll spend the rest of your life being whatever the fucker wants."

He runs his tongue along the lobe of my ear.

"But lucky for you, I want to play with you before I take you back." His grip tightens slightly. "But don't pretend this means something. Don't get any wild ideas about my saving you. That's not happening."

"I know what you are."

"Do you?" His eyes meet mine. "Because I'm your devil and I'm about to use the fuck out of your body."

He can think that if he wants. But I know what this is. And I'm the one using him.

"So tell me, Briar." His free hand trails down my side. "Is that really what you want?"

"Yes." I force myself to stand tall, staring into his stormy eyes. "I want you to use me. And I don't care what that makes me."

He smiles. The bastard actually smiles like he just won some victory.

Well, take your fucking prize, Cain.

"Good girl." His voice is rougher than it was a second ago. Like the control is costing him something. "This fucking sundress has to go."

CHAPTER 4

CAIN

She's staring at me like I'm about to break her.

And she's not wrong. I've been waiting hours for this.

I release her throat, and she yanks the dress over her head. The fabric catches on her breasts before she tugs it free.

She's wearing white cotton panties. No bra. Those perfect tits are on display, nipples already hard.

Fuck, I want to ruin her.

She reaches for the panties, and I shake my head.

"Not yet." I grab her throat again and pull her close. "Come here."

I fist my other hand in her hair and kiss her hard. Biting her bottom lip until she gasps, then deepening the kiss when her mouth opens. I can't remember the last time I kissed anyone. Or wanted to, for that matter. Kissing isn't required for fucking, but I couldn't help myself. And she tastes far too good. So fucking sweet.

She tries to take control, and I tighten my grip in her hair until she stops fighting. Until she just takes what I give her.

That's what I want. Submission. Briar Whitmore melting from my touch.

My hand roams down her chest, cupping her breast and then pinching her nipple hard enough to make her whimper. That sound shoots straight to my cock. I want to hear it again. I want to make her whimper and moan and scream until she forgets that bastard husband of hers.

I move down to her hip, gripping hard enough to leave marks. Then around to squeeze her ass to pull her body against mine.

I've been hard for hours thinking about this. About having her at my mercy to do with as I please. About making her come until she breaks.

I spin her so her back is against my chest, one arm across her waist while my other hand slides into the front of her panties.

She's soaking wet and dripping.

"Fuck, you're drenched." I slide two fingers through her slit, circling her clit but not giving her what she needs. Just enough to make her hips buck. "Been thinking about this all day, haven't you? Been sitting in that car soaking these panties while you wanted me."

"Yes," she gasps.

Her hips buck again, seeking more pressure. I pull back slightly and make her chase after my touch.

My cock is throbbing against my jeans, painfully I might add, but I ignore it. Teasing her comes first. I want her so destroyed she can't remember her own name.

"Please, Cain—"

"Please what?" I bite down on her neck, sucking hard. Marking her so she'll see it tomorrow and remember who made her feel this way. "Use your words, little dove. Tell me what you need."

"Please touch me, please make me come—"

"Not yet." I pull my hand away entirely, loving the desperate sound she makes. "You don't get to come until I say so. Until I've had my fill of watching you beg."

She whimpers, and the sound goes straight to my cock.

"You're going to remember every second of this." I bring my wet fingers to her mouth. "Taste yourself. Taste how fucking desperate you are for me."

She does, her tongue sliding over my fingers, and watching her taste herself makes my cock strain hard against my jeans. This is better than I imagined. Having her here, eager to please me.

I shove my fingers deeper into her mouth as her head pushes back against my chest. I can see her eyes watering, but she doesn't stop sucking.

"Good girl," I whisper against her brow as I pull my fingers away.

That's what I want. Her desperate for whatever I will give her. Willing to do whatever I ask because she trusts that I'm going to make it feel like what she's never had before.

I spin her around and kiss her again. I can taste a hint of her pussy on her tongue, and I almost lose control.

Breaking the kiss, I throw her over my shoulder. I grip her ass as I walk her into the bedroom and toss her onto the bed.

She's on her back, and I grab her thighs and spread them wide so I can see her shaven pussy glistening for me.

"Stay like this. Don't fucking move."

She nods, and the sight of her spread open for me makes me want to skip straight to fucking her. But she's not getting off that easily.

I lay over her and kiss her again before I move down her body, biting marks into her skin as I go. Claiming her as mine. Making sure she'll see reminders tomorrow that someone finally gave her what she needed. When I reach her breasts, I take my time. Tongue and teeth on each nipple until she's panting and squirming.

Her fingers settle in my hair, trying to guide me lower.

I catch both wrists and pin them above her head. “Keep them there, or I'll tie you down. And if I have to tie you up, I’m going to make the waiting last even longer.”

“I’ll keep them there, I promise—”

“You better.” I release her wrists and settle between her thighs.

I bury my face in her pussy without warning.

She cries out, and her whole body jerks.

She tastes good. Too fucking good. I could do this for hours. Could make her come on my tongue over and over until she’s begging me to stop. And even then, I’d keep going.

I lick through her slit slowly, deliberately, savoring my first real taste while she gasps above me. After hours of wanting this, I finally have my tongue in her cunt. And it’s better than I thought it would be.

Her hips lift, seeking more, and I press my forearm across her waist to pin her down.

“Stay still. You take what I give you.”

I circle her clit with my tongue with light strokes. Building her up without giving her enough to come.

She's making these sexy, desperate sounds, fighting to stay still like I told her. Her hands stay above her head, fingers curling into fists with the effort of not reaching for me.

She's learning. Learning to obey. Learning that I'm in control and she doesn't get relief until I decide to give it. And watching her learn and submit to me, my cock throbs harder. Makes me want to give her everything and deny her all at once.

I keep the pressure maddening, never quite enough. Watching her breathing get ragged, and her thighs shake.

She's close and I can feel it in how her body tenses, how her pussy clenches around my finger.

I pull back completely.

She sobs, and the sound is desperate.

"No, please, Cain, don't stop, I was so close—"

"Too bad." I press a kiss to her inner thigh, then bite down. "I can feel this greedy cunt trying to take what I haven't allowed yet."

I tease her with my tongue down her slit and then work her clit again while I slide one finger inside her.

I don't think I'll ever get tired of this.

My cock aches, reminding me I want to be inside her, but not yet. Not until she's completely broken down and I've wrung every ounce of control from her body.

She's getting close again. Body tensing, thighs shaking, those desperate little sounds getting louder.

I stop and pull back completely.

"Cain, please, I can't—"

"You can, and you will. You're going to wait until I allow you to come."

Her hands fly down, reaching for me, trying to push my head back to her pussy.

I shift off the bed, grab my belt from the floor, and loop it around her wrists. I guide her bound hands back above her head.

"I warned you." I check the binding to make sure it's tight enough to hold but not cut off circulation. "Do it again, and I strap them to the bedpost. I'll decide when you've earned the right to come."

She's crying now, with frustrated tears streaming down her face.

This is what I wanted. Her completely at my mercy. And seeing her cry from need makes my cock throb.

I settle between her thighs again. Building her up slowly so she's right to the edge and then pulling back again.

"Please, Cain, please—"

I do it again. And again. Each time she gets close, I stop. Each time the begging gets more desperate. But the more I bring her to the edge, the more I feel my control slipping, watching her like this, begging and...completely mine.

She's incoherent now and begging in broken sentences that I barely understand.

"Please, Cain, I need to come. I can't take it anymore. Please let me come. I'll do anything."

Her hands are still bound above her head. Tears stream down her face. And I'm the one who made her pussy swollen and wet.

The satisfaction that gives me is primal and possessive, and I need to get myself under control because this isn't supposed to feel like this.

I slide my hand lower, circling her ass with one finger. Testing and watching her reaction.

She jumps at my touch.

"Did you know it can also feel good if I fuck you here?" I already know she has no clue. Her fuckwad of a husband made nothing feel good for her and probably ensured it hurt.

She makes a pleading whimper and shakes her head.

"I could show you what it's supposed to feel like." I press slightly, just enough pressure for the tip of my finger to enter the puckered hole. "How good it can be when you're properly prepared. Would you want that, little dove?"

I lower my head and run my tongue around the tight opening and barely press the tip inside before pulling back. "Want me to fuck this tight ass and show you it doesn't have to hurt?"

Another series of moans pours out of her, and I'm getting harder just thinking about it. About taking her there. About being the first person to make any of this feel good for her.

"I'd make you beg for it first. And you would." I press the tip of my finger into her ass again, watching her reaction. I won't take her there now, but if I had lube, I might not hold back.

I shift and push two fingers inside her pussy and curl them, finding that spot that makes her whole body jerk, and seal my lips around her clit.

"Please," she begs, the word coming out as two syllables.

I can't make her wait any longer. "Come for me now, Briar," I growl into her pussy before sucking her clit again.

She comes hard and screams my name loud enough that if we weren't isolated in the middle of nowhere, someone would hear.

Her body locks up, then shakes so violently I have to hold her hips down to keep her in place. Her pussy clamps down on my fingers, and the sounds she's making—half scream, half sob—are the best thing I've ever heard.

If my cock weren't bound tight in my jeans, it might even make me come.

I ignore the pain between my legs, and my mouth is on her pussy again. I want to make her come until she passes out from it.

I work her through the first orgasm straight into a second, using my fingers and mouth against her attempts to shift her body. Her pussy clamps down again and again, and the sounds she's making are wrecking what's left of my control. I'm harder than I've ever been, aching to be inside her, but I keep going because watching her fall apart is addictive.

She's sobbing, overwhelmed, trying to close her legs, but I hold them open. I'm already building her toward a third because I can't stop. I don't fucking want to.

I work her through the oversensitivity. Fingers massaging that spot inside while my tongue works her swollen clit. She's begging me to stop and keep going in the same breath.

"Too much, can't, please, don't stop, Cain—"

"You can take it. You're going to take it. One more and then I'll fuck you, little dove." And I need to be inside her. I need to feel her come on my cock the way she's coming on my fingers and tongue.

The third orgasm rips through her even harder than the first two.

I pull back and watch her gasp for air. She's trembling and completely wrecked. Tears soak her face.

She looks at me, and the way her eyes meet mine. It makes my heart race. The urge to claim her and make her mine is stronger than anything I've ever felt before.

Like she belongs to me. Like I have a claim on her beyond the next couple of days.

I flip her over and pull her up onto her knees. She's shaking so hard she can barely hold position with her tied wrists out in front of her and the side of her cheek on the mattress.

"That's it, good girl. Such a pretty pussy. Show me where I'm about to fuck you."

I strip off my clothes, and my cock is finally free. I grab a condom from my wallet and roll it on, positioning myself behind her where I can see how wet and swollen she is for me.

Nothing has ever been more perfect.

What the fuck? I'm not some sentimental asshole. I want her on display and vulnerable. Mine to use however I want.

I need to be inside her, and can't wait another second. I push into her in one brutal thrust.

She moans, and I catch her hips, holding her steady.

"Fuck." The word comes out rough. She's tight. So fucking tight. "You feel that? Feel how deep I am? Feel how perfectly this pussy fits around my cock?"

And nothing has ever felt so good. Like her body was made to take me. The thought shouldn't hit me this hard, but it does.

I pull out slowly, then slam back in. Setting a brutal pace because if I don't, I'm going to fucking come. And I need this to last. I need to feel her cunt squeezing my cock as long as I can.

"Take it, good girl." I pound her while she moans my name over and over. Fuck, I love that sound. "Take every fucking inch. This is what you've been desperate for all day, isn't it? My cock inside you, fucking you the way you need."

I fuck her harder, one hand gripping her hip while the other reaches around to find her clit. She's so sensitive that even a light touch makes her jerk and whimper.

"Come again. Come on my cock."

"I can't, please, I can't take another—"

"You can." I circle her clit roughly, feeling her pussy clench around me. "Come on my cock or I'll keep going until you pass out. Your choice, little dove."

After a few more circles of her clit, she obeys and her pussy clamps down so hard I nearly lose control right there. I have to grit my teeth to keep from finishing.

I will not last much longer. Not with her pussy gripping me like this, not with those sounds she's making. But I need one more. I need to feel her come on my cock one more time.

I pull her up so her back is against my chest, one arm wrapped around her waist to hold her steady. My other hand pulls the belt loose so her hands are free, and then I wrap my hand around her throat to hold her against me while I fuck her from behind.

"Does that feel good, little dove?"

"Yes—"

"Who's making you feel this? Who's the only man who's ever made you come?"

"Cain, you, only you—"

"Not good enough. I want to hear you scream it."

"Cain!"

My control is almost gone. Been on edge for hours, and now that I'm inside her, buried deep, feeling her shake and clench around me, I'm barely holding on.

I want to tell her she'll only think of me anytime someone fucks her, but the thought of anyone touching her makes my breathing erratic, and I fuck her harder.

Her hands have come up behind her and wrap around my neck.

I should pin her to the bed and tie her ass up while I finish fucking her. But her fingers tugging at my hair feels good.

Still, I can't allow her to think she's controlling this. I grip her throat tighter, and pull most of the way out of her and stop.

"Beg me to fuck you, Briar."

"Cain..."

She tries to push back to take my cock, but I hold her in place.

"If you want it, little dove, you are going to have to plead with me to fuck this pussy. And if you stop, I stop."

“Cain, please.” It comes out as a whisper. “Please fuck me. I need it, please.”

I thrust into her hard and set a rhythm to her moans. She moans combinations of “please” and “Cain” over and over as I plow her from behind.

“Can I please come?” The words come out as moans.

”Such a good fucking girl for asking.” I thrust into her hard. “Come on my cock.”

She does almost immediately, clamping down on me as she comes. As soon as her body slumps, I pull out. I rip off the condom and urge her forward.

I come harder than I ever have in my life. The only thing that would have been better is if it had been inside her so I could watch my cum leak out of her pussy. But I release stream after hot white stream across her back and ass.

She’s fucking mine.

The possessive urge I feel for her is so intense I can hardly breathe. Watching my cum paint her skin satisfies something primal in me.

She collapses all the way forward onto the bed, catching her breath as she lies on her stomach.

I grab a washcloth from the bathroom, and dampen it. Settling beside her, I run the cloth over her skin to remove where I came on her.

"You were such a good girl for me," I tell her as I get the rest of her skin clean. I'm not a total fucking dick. And she wasn't just good. She was goddamn addictive.

And I'm going to take her pussy again as soon as I catch my fucking breath. I'm going to take her again and again, because something about her has unleashed a hunger that I'm not sure I can ever satisfy.

When I'm done cleaning her, I rise from the bed to put the washcloth away. But her hand shoots out and grabs my wrist. Her eyes are half-closed, already falling asleep.

"Don't go," she mumbles. "Stay with me."

I don't intend to. But now I should. I don't fucking cuddle, and this wasn't part of the deal. Every second with her, the situation becomes more precarious. I should have left her tied up.

And because I am already claimed by my addiction, I settle onto the bed beside her. She immediately curls up next to me. Before I know what's happening, her head is on my chest.

She makes a small satisfied sound and then she's out, breathing in long even breaths. Fuck, it does things to me. I tighten my arm around her and wonder how the fuck I let any of this happen.

I lie there, staring at the ceiling, her warm body pressed against mine. I listen to her breath, amazed that she feels safe to lay this way with me.

This wasn't supposed to happen. She was supposed to be a job. Retrieve and deliver. Nothing more. But somewhere between the motel room in Nevada and this cabin, something changed.

Hearing her scream my name...it rewired something in me.

I could try to tell myself it's just good sex. Just scratching an itch. But lying here with her curled against me, feeling how perfect she feels in my arms—I'd fucking kill anyone who tried to touch her.

And that's how I know I'm fucked.

My phone buzzes from the pocket of my jeans, and I carefully reach for it on the floor without disturbing her.

I unlock it and see the text notification.

GARRETT: New orders from the council. Roland Whitmore's will instructs his widow to be eliminated. Kill order issued.

I read it again.

Kill order issued.

They expect me to kill her. The woman currently asleep in my arms, whom I've spent the last couple of hours pleasuring and fucking. The women I somehow accidentally gave a piece of myself to.

I'm supposed to fucking murder her.

My phone buzzes again.

GARRETT: Confirm execution within 2 hours and backup will arrive to assist with the body.

I look down at Briar. She's still curled against me, one hand resting on my chest. Bruises forming on her hips where I gripped her. The flush hasn't faded from her skin. She looks peaceful and safe. Like she trusts me for some unknown fucking reason.

And they want her dead.

Within two hours, I'm supposed to confirm I killed her.

I hold her tighter to me.

No.

I can't kill her.

I've killed for them before without hesitation. I don't particularly enjoy it, but it's the job. And I've never gone against an order.

But putting a bullet in her head while she cries and begs for her life, or even while she's sleeping peacefully after I used her perfect body is just not something I'm prepared to do.

I won't fucking do it.

She's had a shit life. And they want to execute her because some dead bastard filed paperwork saying she should die because he did.

Fuck them. Fuck all the goddamn Ravens.

But if I don't kill her, they'll send others. They'll come after both of us.

And that means only one thing.

We run.

We run against the Ravens. Against my family. Against the oath I swore as a Talon. Fuck it all.

My father will be furious. Not just at me, but at what this does to our family's reputation. Decades of loyalty, of proving ourselves reliable, of building trust with the founding families—I'm about to destroy all of it.

All because I won't kill one runaway widow.

I look down at her again. She shifts slightly in her sleep, pressing closer to me. Seeking warmth as her bare skin has goosebumps on it.

It was my job to take her back, and now it's my job to take her away.

I don't need more time to consider it. The decision has been made, and there will be no turning back.

I log into a couple of my bank accounts and transfer as much money as I can to my offshore accounts. Fortunately, I already have a lot of money there. We'll need to get cash as soon as we can.

I toss the phone onto the floor after I'm done. I won't take that with me. We'll have to get a new vehicle right away in case mine has a tracking device.

We must leave immediately. I need to get her somewhere safe. Somewhere the Ravens can't find her and I can keep her safe.

She's been my captive for two days—just two days—and somehow she became the thing I won't sacrifice.

I must be out of my fucking mind.

But the alternative...watching the life leave her eyes. No way in hell am I doing that.

I stare at her long blonde hair splayed down her back and her head settled on my chest.

I'm not giving her up. Not to the Ravens. Not to anyone.

I don't even know why Roland wanted her dead. But Garrett knew this might happen. This explains why he changed the plan for where we'd stop each night. He wanted me to take her to the woods to make it easier to kill her if needed.

I should have suspected, but she's had me distracted since she walked out of that motel bathroom the first day, gorgeous and spitting fire.

Fuck.

I remember the car on our way to the cabin. I wondered if they were following us. And they may be the backup that is on standby to take her body. Which means we don't have much time.

"Briar," I brush her hair from her face. "Wake up. We have to go."

"Go?" She's groggy and still half asleep. "It's still dark."

"Briar," I say again, climbing from the bed and bringing her with me. "Get dressed now."

I can explain it to her in the car. Every minute we wait costs us a step ahead of the Ravens.

"Cain." My name comes out as a whine. It makes me want to tie her to the bed and remind her who is in control here. But I set her on her feet.

I pick up her dress and hand it to her. Then I grab my underwear.

"If you want to be free from the Ravens, you will do every fucking thing I say and not ask questions until I tell you that you can."

Her eyes widen, and then she slips her sundress over her head. She opens her mouth as if she might ask a question and then closes it again.

Briar nods her agreement and then picks up her panties from the floor.

We both finish dressing, and I grab our bags we never unpacked. I unzip mine to check my handgun and ammo in the case. I take the gun and check that it's loaded and shove a handful of the ammo in my pocket.

"Cain..."

There are tears running down her cheeks, and she's holding her arms across her body while she trembles.

I set the bags down and tuck the gun in the back of my jeans. I walk over to her and pull her into my arms.

I place a light kiss on the top of her head. "Just get in the car, little dove."

I'm protecting her now.

And if any fucking Raven thinks to lay a hand on her, they are fucking dead.

CHAPTER 5

BRIAR

I don't say a word for the first several minutes as Cain's SUV speeds down the country roads.

Cain told me not to ask questions until he said I could, and I'm not stupid enough to test him right now. Not when his hands are gripping the steering wheel hard enough to make his knuckles white. He's checking the mirrors every thirty seconds like he expects something to materialize behind us.

My heart hasn't stopped racing since he shook me awake. As soon as I saw his face, I knew something was very wrong.

He turns down another dark road.

"Can I ask questions now?" I finally say.

He glances at me. "Yes."

"What's happening?"

"The Ravens want you dead." He growls the words. "The kill order came through while you were asleep. I'm supposed to confirm when it's done."

My stomach drops so fast I think I might throw up.

"You're supposed to—" I can't finish the sentence.

"Kill you. Yes." He takes a sharp left turn without slowing down. "I'm not going to."

My throat tightens. But I refuse to allow myself to cry.

"Why would they want me dead? I thought I was going to auction. You said—"

"Plans changed." His jaw is tight enough that I can see the muscle ticking. "Roland put something in his will. Apparently he ordered that if he dies, you die too."

The words make little sense at first. My brain keeps trying to rearrange them into something that does.

Roland hated me so much that even in death, he wants me dead too.

While I was sleeping in his bed, while I was trying to be a good wife, while I was convincing myself that the broken ribs were my fault for making him angry—he was planning to take me with him to the grave.

I remember what he used to say. That I'd never have a life outside of him. That I belonged to him forever, and that even death wouldn't change that.

I thought he was being cruel and intimidating. It turns out the bastard meant it literally.

"He knew I'd likely outlive him, and he never wanted me to have a chance at a life."

"Yeah. He was a sick fuck."

The casual way Cain says it almost makes me laugh. Almost.

"So you decided we would run?"

"That's the situation." He keeps his eyes fixed on the road.

I turn in my seat to look at him. His shoulders rise and fall from how hard he's breathing. And his expression is one that could kill.

"You are throwing your entire life away for me."

"Yes."

"They're going to come after you. Your family, the other Talons—"

"I know." He cut me off. "I know exactly what they're going to do because I've been on the other side of this hunt. That's why we're going to stay ahead of them."

"For how long?"

"Long enough." He checks the mirror again. "Unless you'd prefer I turn around and finish the job."

"Fuck you."

"Then stop questioning decisions that are already made." His tone softens just slightly. "We're running. Together. Everything else we figure out as we go."

I stare out the windshield at the road disappearing into darkness. My kidnapper just chose me over his entire life.

The man who pinned me against a wall and made me beg. He fucked me like he owned me and then held me while I slept.

I had lain in his arms, dreaming that he wouldn't take me back. That he'd keep me as his own. If a fairy godmother is granting wishes, next time I need to be more specific. Because this isn't exactly what I had in mind.

But Cain just burned down his entire future rather than see me dead.

"You could have followed orders," I whisper.

"Yeah. I suppose I could have."

I'm annoying him. But I don't care.

"So why didn't you?"

He's quiet for a long moment. I want the answer to the question. I need to know.

"Because reading that text telling me to execute you made me want to put my fist through a wall," he finally says. "Because the idea of following that order made me want to set the entire fucking world on fire. And because I decided that you're mine now. The Ravens don't get to take what's mine."

The way he says "mine" makes me shiver.

"Yours?" I repeat.

"Yeah, you're mine." He says it as if it's the most obvious thing in the world. "I claimed you. I made you come on my cock. It's my name on your lips. That makes you mine, not theirs. And I don't hand over what belongs to me just because someone sends a fucking text message."

I don't care if it's toxic as fuck. His words only make me want him more.

His hands tighten on the wheel. "And anyone who tries to take you from me is going to find out exactly what that means."

"But the Ravens—"

"Fuck the Ravens." He glances at me, and there's something dark and possessive in his eyes. "You're mine now, Briar. And I will kill anyone who looks at you wrong."

I should be scared. This is a man who is trained to kill, and he's claiming ownership of me. Roland believed he owned me, too.

But it's not the same. Roland owned me like property. I wasn't any more to him than a piece of furniture. At least he allowed his furniture to be sold when he died.

Cain owns me like I'm something precious. I'm someone worth burning down his entire world to keep.

"You're not my captor anymore." I turn in my seat to face him fully. "You think you're the only one making a choice here?"

His jaw tightens. "Briar—"

"I'm choosing you too, you possessive asshole." The words come out fiercely. "You're mine just as much as I'm yours. So if the Ravens try to kill you, they're going to have to go through me. Got it?"

He reaches out and grabs the back of my neck, pulling me across the center console.

Then he kisses me. His other hand stays steady on the wheel, keeping us on the road, but his mouth on mine, hungrily taking what he wants, is everything I need.

It's far too quick. He releases me and refocuses on the road.

"Let's be clear about something," he growls. "Your life is more important than mine. I'm the one in control here. And when I tell you to do something, you do it. Understand?"

"But—"

"No fucking 'buts,' Briar. You do as I say. Do you understand?"

My pulse is racing under his palm. "Yes. But I don't want anything to happen to you."

"I know what I'm doing."

His right hand drops to my thigh and stays there. It feels right. Like I was always meant to be his.

He keeps driving like this is perfectly normal. I could pretend we're just a normal couple out joyriding instead of what we really are.

Who fucking knows what we are? He kidnapped me a few days ago, and now there is no chance that I could let him go.

I claimed him as mine. And I meant it.

And my body woke up for him in ways it never had before. Not just sexually. It's everything. I feel alive around him. This feels far more normal and right than eight years married to an old man because my father arranged it. This is my choice.

Is that love? I don't know. And I don't care.

It's something. It's real and raw. Maybe it's a lot of fucked up.

And I'm choosing him anyway.

His hand squeezes my thigh gently. It's like he needs the contact as much as I do.

We drive in silence for a few more hours.

He pulls off at a sketchy car lot where he trades the SUV for an old sedan. He gave the man the keys to the SUV and a wad of cash and then moved our bags to the sedan.

The sedan isn't nearly as nice as his SUV. The seats are worn, there's a rattle coming from somewhere under the hood, and I'm pretty sure the air conditioning hasn't worked for more than a decade.

But it's untraceable. That's what matters.

Cain made stops at a few different banks and kept me close while he made large withdrawals. I know he comes from money. He couldn't be a Talon and not come from a rich family.

We stop only for gas and food. Our diet is basically whatever the country gas stations have on their hot bar.

Cain wants to avoid being seen on cameras that the Ravens could tap into, so we have to avoid major roads and cities.

Each stop is ten minutes at most. We fill the gas tank, get a snack, and use the bathroom. One of the gas stations is next to a dollar store, and he took me there to grab jeans and tank tops.

They aren't designer labels like I've worn my entire life, and I don't give a fuck. I'm more excited about dollar store jeans than I've ever been for any of the Couture gowns I had to wear for Raven events.

After each stop, his hand always returns to my thigh. And it feels right. I know I belong at Cain's side.

The sun set a couple of hours ago. Ahead there is a sign for a motel. It's like one of those horror movies where a couple of letters no longer light and the building looks like the kind of place where someone gets murdered.

And Cain pulls off the road and into the parking lot.

"We're stopping?" I sit up straighter. "Shouldn't we keep moving?"

"We've been driving for hours. We need to get a bit of rest." He parks in front of the office. "A few hours of sleep now means we're sharper if we have a situation to deal with."

"Are you sure it's safe here?"

"Don't forget who you have protecting you." He almost sounds offended. "And I'd rather not risk having any issues at night. Nothing is open overnight in these small towns."

He's right. I hate it, but he's right.

The motel clerk takes Cain's cash without looking up from his phone. Cain requested the room at the end of the row.

Cain uses the key and ushers me inside. He sets the bags on the bed and immediately tests the locks and checks the bathroom. He peers out the window and watches for a few moments and then closes the curtains.

He goes to his bag and pulls out a big metal device. He wedges it under the door handle and secures it in place.

"What is that?" I ask.

"Insurance." He tests it. "No one's bursting through the door without equipment."

"You just carry that with you? What else do you have in that bag of yours?"

He turns to face me. "The things I need to do my job."

I don't need to know anything else.

"What do we do now? Just go to sleep?"

"You need to shower," he says. And it doesn't sound like a suggestion.

"Is that an order?"

His eyes meet mine. And just looking at him does things to me.

"Yes."

Fuck, why does he have to make me want him so much?

"I'd be safer if you showered with me."

"I fully intended to." He grabs my hand and pulls me with him toward the bathroom.

He leaves the bathroom door open and turns on the water, running his hand under the steam to check the temperature. He pulls the gun from the back of his jeans and sets it on the counter near the shower.

A car door slams outside, and we both freeze.

Cain grabs the gun, and he motions for me to stay in the bathroom while he creeps back to the room and peeks out the curtain.

My heart pounds so loud I'm sure he can hear it.

I hear footsteps moving away from our room. Then a door opens and closes down the row.

He returns to the bathroom and sets the gun back on the counter.

"Get undressed," he commands. "We need to be quick."

I take a few seconds to pull off the dress and then remove my panties.

His eyes move over my body, and then he nods toward the shower. "Get in."

I step under the spray. The water is hot and feels good.

Cain strips and I get a good look at his muscular body. I didn't get to explore his body much last night, and seeing him now in the bright fluorescent bathroom lighting is making my knees weak. He's all defined lines from how toned he is.

Fuck. And he's mine.

Then he steps in behind me. The shower isn't all that big, so we're pressed close together. His cock is already hard against my back.

"Turn around and face me, little dove."

I do, and he reaches for the motel shampoo. His hands work through my hair, his strong fingers massaging my scalp. It's almost as good as an orgasm.

He has me lean my head back into the water and helps to rinse my hair. Then, he uses the little bar of soap and lathers his hands. He runs them over my shoulders and down my arms.

He keeps going. When he cups my breasts, his thumbs brush over my nipples, and I gasp.

"Stay still," he murmurs. "You're not done."

His hands continue their path. Down my stomach. Over my hips. Between my thighs.

One finger slides through my opening, and I'm already wet for him.

"Still my needy girl," he says with satisfaction. "This pussy belongs to me now."

"Yes," I breathe.

When he's finally done cleaning me, he takes the bar of soap again and uses the soap on himself.

I take the soap from him. "My turn."

We might get killed at any moment, and if I'm going to die, at least I got to touch his perfect body one more time.

I lather my hands and then start with his chest. I work my way down his body, washing him as I go.

When I reach his cock, I wrap my soapy hand around it.

He groans. "Briar—"

I stroke him slowly. "I'm just washing you."

His hand braces against the wall. "That's you being a tease."

"Maybe I want to make you feel as desperate as you make me feel."

"Fuck." His jaw clenches when I squeeze tighter. "You're going to pay for this."

I sink to my knees on the shower floor and look up at him, watching the water run down his sexy body. "Promise?"

I close my mouth around his cock. He's huge, and I can't take all of him, but I do my best. The water makes it harder for me to breathe, but I don't let up.

His hand fists in my wet hair.

"That's it. Swallow my cock." He groans. "Fuck, you look good on your knees for me."

I hollow my cheeks and take him deeper. My hand strokes the base of what I can't fit into my mouth.

This is what power feels like, and it's intoxicating. Knowing that I hold my dangerous captor's pleasure in my hands. That I choose to kneel for him.

"That's a good girl. Sucking my cock so well. We'll have my entire dick in your mouth with practice." His breathing is ragged. "You like this, don't you?"

I moan around him in response.

A door slams outside, and we both freeze. Him in my mouth. My hands on his thighs.

There are voices outside. But then there is laughter, and they fade away.

Cain withdraws from my mouth and pulls me to stand.

"I said we needed to be quick." His voice is rough with need. "And I need to fuck you. Right now."

He reaches out of the shower and in a few seconds returns with a wrapped condom. He hands it to me and then picks me up. I wrap my legs around his waist, and my back is against the shower wall.

"Put the condom on me," he commands.

I fumble with the package and then finally tear it open and position it on his cock, then roll it down his length.

He's watching my face. "You know what to do next, little dove."

I don't hesitate. "Fuck me, Cain."

He lifts me up, and I guide him to my opening as he lowers my body down so I take all of him.

"Cain," I moan.

"Fuck, you are perfect." He grips my hips and thrusts into me, moving my hips as he fucks me into the shower wall. "This tight pussy was made for my cock."

I grab his head and pull his lips to mine while my body is bouncing hard on his cock.

He sets a brutal rhythm, fucking me hard as I tighten my legs to hold on.

"Briar," Cain says against my lips. "No one is going to take you from me."

Water runs over both of us. His hands grip my ass, fingers digging in hard enough to leave marks. Good. I want his marks all over my body.

"Tell me who you belong to," he growls. "Say it."

"You. I belong to you."

"That's right. Mine." He thrusts harder. Deeper. "Mine to fuck. Mine to protect. Mine."

I'm far too close already. "Yes. I'm yours, Cain."

One of his hands slides between us and finds my clit. He circles it with his finger.

"Come for me," he commands. "Come on my cock right now."

His fingers work my clit while his cock drives deep.

"Now, Briar."

My orgasm hits so hard I see stars. I bury my face in his neck and bite down to muffle the sounds. My whole body clenches around him, not wanting to ever let him go.

He fucks me through it with quick, desperate thrusts. Then he groans low, and I feel him pulse inside me.

We stay like that for a moment. Both catching our breath.

Finally, he lifts me off of him and lowers me to my feet. My legs fucking shake.

He turns off the water and grabs a towel. He dries himself and then fixes the towel low on his hips. Then he picks up his gun and checks the room again.

Right. Back to reality. Back to being hunted.

I step out of the shower, and he returns to hand me a towel without taking his eyes off the door.

"Get dressed, little dove," he says quietly. "Put on the jeans and tank top in case we need to leave quickly."

I grab the bag with my new clothes. After eight years of Roland controlling every piece of clothing I wore, nothing but dresses, it feels monumental.

I dry off and pull on the underwear first. Then the jeans. They feel strange against my skin, but freeing at the same time.

I don't have a clean bra, so I pull on the tank top and look at myself in the foggy mirror.

I look nothing like the perfect Dove wife I was trained to be.

When I come out, Cain is already dressed and standing near the window.

His eyes move over me slowly when he sees me in jeans for the first time. I turn for him like I'm putting on a fashion show, and I notice how his gaze lingers on my ass.

"How do they feel?" he asks.

"Different. Good different."

"You look good in them." His voice is rough. "Really fucking good."

"Better than a sundress?"

"Fuck that sundress." He crosses over to me. His hands settle on my hips, then slide around to cup my ass. "This ass in jeans is going to be a problem for me."

"A problem?"

"Yeah. Because all I'm going to think about is peeling these off you." He squeezes and then gives me a playful smack. "It's going to drive me insane."

Good. He deserves to be as crazy as he makes me.

He pulls back the covers and urges me to climb into the bed.

"Will you at least lie down with me?"

He's quiet for a moment. Then he sets the gun on the nightstand and follows me into the bed, pulling the covers over us.

I settle against his chest and just listen to his heartbeat for several minutes.

"Will you really kill anyone who comes after us?"

His arm tightens around me. "If they try to take you, yes. Without hesitation."

"Even if it's someone important to you? I'm sure some Talons were your friends."

"You're what's important to me now." He says it simply. Like it's just a fact. "And no friend of mine would try to kill either of us. You're my partner in this now. We're going to fight every mother fucker they send after us."

I nod against his chest, fighting sleep. "I know we will," I say through a yawn.

"Sleep," Cain murmurs. "I've got you."

I let my eyes close. Everything is terrifying and fucked up. And we might not live past tomorrow.

But right now, there is no place I'd rather be than in Cain's arms.

CHAPTER 6

CAIN

She's asleep in my arms, and I'm mentally planning how I'm going to kill Keegan.

It's not *if* I have to, but *when* I do.

Keegan will come first. He trained me, which means he knows how I think. That makes him the most dangerous. The Ravens will send him because he's all business, and he doesn't let personal feelings impede the job.

The way I used to be.

Too bad for him, I've gotten very fucking personal about this particular job. And I have no choice. It's them or us.

I shift slightly on the bed, careful not to wake her. Briar's head is on my chest, one hand curled against my ribs. Even in sleep, she looks nothing like the terrified widow I pulled out of that Nevada motel.

And she's fucking mine.

I threw away everything for her. My family's reputation. My standing with the Ravens. Years of building trust and proving myself worthy of the assholes.

And I'd do it again without hesitation.

Not because I'm some hero. I'm not that guy. Never have been. I'm selfish as fuck, and what I want is her.

Briar shifts in her sleep, pressing closer. Her leg slides between mine. Even in sleep, she knows who she belongs to.

I tighten my arm around her and scan the room again. The door is secure, and the window is locked.

But we can't stay here long. They are out there, and I'd rather have control of how this all goes down.

The Ravens don't accept failure or disobeying orders. And they sure as hell don't accept one of their own Talons going rogue to protect a target.

They'll send everyone they can spare until both of us are dead.

I've gone on this mission before. I've ended a fellow Talon's life for their failure to comply.

If I'm being realistic about the odds, it's going to be a tough fight.

But I'm taking as many of them with me as I can. And Briar is walking away from this alive even if I don't.

That's the only outcome I'll accept.

My hand slides down to her hip. The denim is rough under my palm. I like her in jeans. I like that she picked them out herself, and that every time she looks in a mirror, she'll remember that I'm the one who gave her the freedom to choose.

I'm the one who will kill for her. I burned down my entire life, so my girl gets to wear whatever the fuck she wants.

Roland thought he owned her. But he was just a pathetic bastard who needed to control a woman to feel like a man. He broke her down because he was too weak to handle a woman with fire.

I don't need to break her. And submitting to me is very different from what she survived with him.

I'm a domineering asshole. But with me, she's cared for, fucked properly, and kept alive. I still don't really understand what's going on in my head and why I can't let her go.

Or why she chose me.

Her breathing changes slightly. She's waking up.

"How long was I out?" Her voice is rough with sleep.

"Twenty minutes. Maybe thirty."

I run my hand up her spine. "We need to move in a couple of hours. I don't want to stay in one place too long until we can cross the border."

She lifts her head to look at me. Her hair is messy, and her eyes are still heavy. "Don't you need to sleep?"

I brush a strand of hair from her face. "Don't you worry about me, little dove."

She sits up. "I can keep watch and you can sleep."

"No." I pull her back down against my chest. I'm not ready to let her go yet. "I'm resting here."

She goes quiet for a moment and then picks up her head to look at me. "Are you really going to kill other Talons? Men you know?"

"Yes."

Briar goes quiet and won't look at me.

"Are you afraid of me now?"

Her eyes finally meet mine, and I can see the intensity there. "No. I just hate that I'm ruining your life and making you do these things."

"My life is far from ruined. I've hated those fucking Ravens, but I didn't see another choice than to do what was expected. Until now." I grip her ass, holding her hard against my hip. "They will make their choice if they come after us, and I made mine when I decided you were worth more than following a fucking cult. Now we deal with the consequences."

"Just like that?"

"Just like that." I press a rough kiss to her lips. "You're what matters now. Everything else is just obstacles in the way of keeping you alive."

We lie there in silence. I should plan our next move. But right now, I'm memorizing everything about the way she feels. The way her breath sounds. The way her hair looks in messy damp waves.

If I die in the next few days, at least I'll die knowing it was to save what is mine.

Better than dying as just another Raven soldier following orders.

"Cain?"

"Yeah?"

"What happens if they catch us?"

"They won't."

"But if they do—"

"Then we fight." I tilt her chin up so she has to look at me. "Together. If you are my partner in this, you follow my instructions. I won't let them take you. Do you understand?"

She nods. "Partners."

I give her another rough kiss. A reminder that she's mine. That I'm keeping her. That she is not a sacrifice in whatever happens.

When I pull back, she releases a satisfied growl and rubs her body along my side.

Good. I want her to be hungry for me. I want her addicted to my touch the way I'm addicted to hers. It's only fucking fair.

"Get some more sleep," I tell her. "I'll wake you when it's time to move."

"What about you?"

"Do as I say, partner." I run my thumb along her jaw. "One of us needs to stay alert. That's me. You need to rest while you can. That's you. Don't argue with me about this."

She opens her mouth to argue anyway, then closes it. Smart girl.

She settles back against my chest and closes her eyes. Within minutes, her breathing evens out.

I don't sleep. I use the time to plan.

We're going to continue heading north over the border, and then I'll access the millions in my foreign accounts and set us up somewhere.

We'll have new identities. New lives. And disappear completely from all the Raven fuckers.

My phone would be blowing up right now if I still had it. Garrett would demand updates. My father probably already called to ask what the fuck I'm thinking. Dane Sinclair, a founding family enforcer, would probably have called me himself, too. He might even send one of his sons after me.

I'd advise against it unless Dane wants to bury his son.

The next two hours pass faster than I'd like, but I have a plan for where we are headed.

"Briar." I brush my lips against her temple. "Time to move."

She groans and buries her face against my chest. "Five more minutes."

"No." I sit up, taking her with me. "We need to go. Now."

She blinks at me, still half asleep. Then awareness kicks in and she's moving.

We're packed and in the car within three minutes. The sedan starts on the second try. Not ideal for a quick getaway vehicle, but it runs well enough. I'll swap out vehicles again today.

"Where to?" Briar asks as I pull out onto the road.

"North. But we have to stay on back roads like we've been doing."

"And then?"

I back the car away from the motel, and we pull back out onto the two-lane road.

"Then we get across the border."

She's quiet for a moment. Then she says, "Is it wrong that I dreamed of you and me in a house together near a beach somewhere?"

I rest my hand on her thigh, needing to touch her, and I actually smile at her. What is this girl doing to me?

"Let's just survive today, and then I'll see about getting you the beach house."

I can feel her watching me as I drive. Then, she covers my hand with hers, lacing our fingers together.

I don't know what this is. I didn't think I was capable of some flowery thing like love. But fuck, if this is what love is, then I'm as fucked as she is. And I don't fucking care.

We drive for two hours holding hands as I watch everything and everyone along the way.

There are checkpoints everywhere. State police are conducting random stops. The reach of the Ravens is endless. They don't normally involve the police, but I can't take any chances.

"Is that another one?" Briar asks.

"Yeah." I turn in a different direction than I had planned. "This could be them, but I can't risk us going through the checkpoint."

"If this is them, they're funneling us to a specific point. They'd want to control where and how the confrontation happens." I check the mirror. Still clear behind us. "It's what I'd do if I were hunting someone. Limit their options until they have to go where I want them."

It's actually a smart strategy. Whoever's coordinating this knows what they're doing. Dane fucking Sinclair has deep connections, and could pull something like this off.

"So, what do we do?"

"We avoid the obvious routes. Take roads they won't expect. Make them work for it." I turn onto an even smaller back road. "But eventually we're going to run out of options. They know that. So do I."

"And then?"

"Then we see if I'm as good as I think I am."

She doesn't respond to that. Just keeps her hand on mine and watches the road.

I wish I had more comforting words for her. But the truth is, it's me against the Ravens. Still, I'm more motivated than any of them.

We drive for another hour. I'm hyperaware of every car that passes. And I reach for my gun at every vehicle that stays in my mirrors too long.

Nothing obvious yet. But they're out there. I can feel it. That prickling awareness that comes from years of being the hunter.

Now, Briar and I are the prey.

Turns out I don't like it much from this side.

"We need gas," Briar says, checking the gauge.

Fuck. She's right. The needle is getting close to being on empty.

I scan ahead. There's a station coming up in a few miles.

"We'll make it quick," I tell her. "Stay in the car. Keep the engine running. If anything feels wrong, you drive away."

"I'm not leaving you—"

"If something happens to me, you run." My voice is harsh. I won't be moved on this. "You drive away and you don't look back. You hear me? That's not a request."

She sets her jaw. "I understand."

"Say it back to me."

"If something happens to you, I run."

"Good girl."

I pull into the station. There are only two other rundown cars in the lot. No sign of anyone from the Ravens.

I glance at the cars again, and the more I look at them, the more something feels off. The cars are parked oddly. And the attendant inside is still in the window, like a mannequin.

I reach to put the car in reverse, and that's when I see it.

A black SUV is pulling in right behind us.

My hand goes right to my gun.

The SUV parks, and three men get out. I recognize the one in front immediately.

Keegan.

This was inevitable. I knew that. But I was hoping for a few more days to get further ahead.

No such luck.

The other two Talons move to flank us. Keegan wouldn't bring anyone who might hesitate to take me down.

Smart of him, but I won't hesitate to take them down either.

Keegan's eyes meet mine across the twenty feet of deserted dirt parking lot. He doesn't look sorry. Doesn't look conflicted. Just determined to complete his mission.

I respect that. I'd feel the same way if our positions were reversed.

I glance at Briar. Her face is red, and her eyes are wide. Fuck, she's still gorgeous.

"Cain. Just drive away now."

I lean over to her and grab her throat to pull her to me, then place a bruising kiss on her lips. "Drive, little dove. After I get out, drive away and don't come back."

"Cain. No."

"Briar—"

"We're partners. We are both going to fight."

"Cain," Keegan calls out. "Don't make this harder than it needs to be."

The other two Talons are in place behind Keegan.

Fuck. "Briar, just fucking drive away."

I release her and step out of the car. Closing the door behind me, I step forward so she has room to escape. I keep my gun behind my back.

I can tell Keegan is doing the same with the way his arm is positioned.

This is it. The moment everything goes to hell.

I move my gun to my side so he can see it. There is no use pretending that this is going to end any other way. I still don't hear the engine start. Goddamnit.

"Last chance," Keegan says. His weapon is still behind his back. "Stand down. Hand her over and come back with us. I'll ask the council to show you both mercy. Dane Sinclair might be willing to see reason."

"We both know that's not happening." I force my voice to remain calm. "She's mine. And you aren't taking her, Keegan."

Keegan's expression hardens. "Then you've made your choice."

"Yes, I fucking have."

Somehow I, Cain Bradley Mercer, am in love with my captive. And I should have fucking told her so before I die.

Keegan raises his weapon, and it's too late for regrets. If she intends to stay, it's even more important that I don't miss.

I point my gun at him.

And I pull the fucking trigger.

CHAPTER 7

BRIAR

Gunshots explode through the air and make my ears ring.

Then everything happens at warp speed.

The one that Cain referred to as Keegan moves impossibly fast for a man who appears to be in his forties. He's already rolling to the side before Cain's bullet hits the pavement where he was standing a second ago.

The other two Talons scatter in opposite directions to take position to target Cain.

We are so completely fucked.

Cain fires again. The bullet catches one of the Talons in the shoulder. The man stumbles but keeps coming, like getting shot is just a minor inconvenience.

Keegan pulls a knife from his pocket and closes the distance to Cain.

Cain dodges the first slash, but the blade still catches his forearm. A trickle of blood runs down his arm.

The other two Talons have appeared on each side of Cain. They've got him boxed in.

It's three trained killers against one man. Even if that man is Cain and even if he's very good at killing people, the math is not working in our favor here.

Cain blocks another knife strike from Keegan. He fights hand-to-hand with Keegan, matching him move for move.

The Talon with the shoulder wound throws a punch that Cain has to block. The distraction is exactly what Keegan needs. He slashes again, and this time the blade catches Cain's shirt across his ribs.

Cain grunts and steps back.

The third Talon circles behind Cain while he's focused on Keegan and the wounded one. Before Cain can react, the man gets him in a chokehold from behind. His arm wraps around Cain's throat.

Cain's hands immediately go to the arm around his neck. He's trying to break the grip so he can breathe. But the Talon holding him is built like a fucking tank and isn't letting go.

Keegan steps forward with the knife raised. "I told you we didn't have to do this the hard way."

Cain's face is turning red. But he hasn't stopped struggling.

He's going to die right here in this shitty gas station parking lot in the middle of nowhere.

The man who promised me a beach house and told me to drive away is going to die.

Drive away, he said. If something happens to me, you run.

Fuck that.

Keegan is raising the knife higher. He says something else to Cain that I can't quite hear, but whatever it is makes Cain fight harder.

I throw open the door and run toward the trunk of the sedan.

There's a tire iron back here. Cain made me memorize where every weapon was hidden when we decided to run.

I pop the trunk and grab the tire iron. The metal is heavier than I expected and cold in my sweating palms. My hands are shaking so hard I almost drop it.

I've never hit anyone with a weapon before. I never once fought back in eight years with Roland. I took every hit.

I run at Keegan with the tire iron raised. My heart is hammering so loudly in my ears that I can barely hear anything else. My hands are shaking, and my legs feel like jelly, but I'm running anyway.

He doesn't see me coming. He's too focused on his smug victory over Cain.

Bad move, asshole.

I swing the tire iron at his knee with everything I have—every ounce of strength, every bit of rage I've been storing up for eight years, every ounce of fear and shame from believing I was Roland's defective, worthless wife.

The impact travels up my arms and makes my shoulders ache. But I hit him again. The sound of metal hitting bone is worse than I imagined.

Keegan goes down screaming. The knife flies from his hand and skitters across the dirt away from both of them.

His knee is bent at an angle that knees definitely should not bend, like someone took his leg and folded it wrong.

I did that.

And I don't feel bad about it for a second.

I feel fucking powerful.

I have never felt freer or more alive. If Cain wants to burn down the entire world, then I'm the one who's going to light the fucking match.

Cain has room to move now. The Talon holding him is distracted by Keegan's screaming. Cain drives his elbow back into the man's ribs. Once. Twice. Three times.

The arm around Cain's throat loosens just enough.

Cain spins in the man's grip and gets his hands on either side of the Talon's head.

He twists hard and fast.

The snap is so loud, like breaking a large branch.

The Talon's lifeless body drops to the ground.

The third Talon is on me before I can process what I just saw.

He grabs for the tire iron, and I swing it at his face instead. I put everything into it—all my fear and desperation to keep Cain and me from dying in this parking lot.

The tire iron cracks across his cheekbone. Blood sprays, but he doesn't stop.

He's much stronger than I am. His hand closes around my throat, and he lifts me off the ground like I weigh absolutely nothing.

My feet are dangling in the air. The weapon falls from my hands and clatters on the pavement. I can't fucking breathe.

I claw at the hand around my throat, but it doesn't do anything.

Black spots crowd the edges of my vision. My lungs are burning and screaming for air that won't come. My vision is tunneling.

This is how I die—after running, after Cain chose me and I chose him back, after I finally felt alive again for the first time in eight years, after I finally found love in the darkness.

My vision has almost blacked out, but I know Cain is there.

I hear a bone crack, and the Talon yells several curses. Then I'm dropped to the ground.

My hip crashes into the dirt. Pain shoots through my entire body, but I can breathe again, and that's all that matters.

I gasp and cough and try not to throw up while sweet air floods into my lungs.

Cain doesn't stop to check on me. He's on the Talon, tackling him to the ground.

Cain gives him three fast, hard hits to the face. His nose is definitely broken. Then he picks the bastard's head up and slams it hard into the ground over and over.

I am certain the man is long dead, but Cain isn't ready to stop taking out his fury.

I see something moving nearby. It's Keegan.

"Cain," I shout. "It's Keegan."

Keegan is trying to crawl away, his shattered knee dragging behind him. He's leaving a trail of blood across the dirt like a wounded animal trying to get to a gun a few feet away.

He makes it a few inches before Cain reaches him. I scramble to my feet and hurry over to kick the gun away.

"Wait—" Keegan looks up at Cain with desperation in his eyes. "Cain, wait. We can talk about this. The Council might listen if you—"

Cain doesn't wait. He doesn't let him finish the sentence.

He grabs Keegan's head with the same grip he used on the other Talon.

"This is for coming after what's mine," Cain snarls at him.

I hear another snap.

Keegan's body goes slack, and his eyes stare at nothing at all.

Cain drops the body and rushes to me. His hands are on my face, and he's checking me over.

"Are you hurt?"

"I'm fine." My voice comes out rough. My throat hurts like hell where the Talon grabbed me. "You're the one bleeding."

"Get in the car. Now." He pulls me to my feet and propels me toward the sedan. "We need to get out of here while we have a chance to get away."

Cain drives fast and doesn't bother to stop at stop signs.

"I told you to drive away," he says without taking his eyes off the road.

"You were being choked to death. What was I supposed to do?"

"Run, and give yourself a better chance to survive." His jaw is tight. "I told you to run if something happened to me."

He glances at me, and something shifts in his expression. "You could have died."

"So could you." I look at the blood soaking through his shirt. "We need to stop that bleeding before you pass out."

"Not yet. We need to ditch this car first. Their SUV probably had cameras."

We drive for fifteen minutes in tense silence. Every car that passes makes my heart race. Every siren in the distance makes me flinch.

He pulls off onto what looks like an old logging road, overgrown and barely visible from the highway.

"One of these should work." He brings the car to a stop beside one of the trucks. "Grab our bags. We shouldn't stay here too long."

We transfer our bags to the truck. Cain wipes down the sedan's interior and steering wheel with his shirt, just in case they don't know the sedan was ours.

He is able to hotwire the truck and get it started. I get out to help transfer the last of our stuff. We're standing between the two vehicles when Cain's eyes lock on mine.

Both of us are covered in blood. And somehow both of us are alive when three trained killers aren't.

"Come here," he says. His voice is rough.

I close the distance between us, and he's on me immediately. His mouth crashes into mine. The kiss is desperate, like he believed he'd never kiss me again.

I know that fear well.

He tries to pull back, but my hands are on his zipper. "I need you. Right now."

Cain groans and pins me into the side of the truck, massaging his tongue hard against mine.

I start to unbutton his jeans, but he pulls my hand away.

"I don't have another condom."

"I don't fucking care. If we can take down three trained assassins, I think I can handle whatever a potential child of yours would throw at me."

"Are you sure?"

"Just fuck me, Cain."

He unbuttons my jeans and jerks them down my legs, bringing my panties with them.

Cain lifts me up and pins me against the side of the truck. His hands find my hair and pull my head back so my neck is exposed to him, allowing him access to suck and bite his way up to my ear.

"Don't forget who's in fucking control here, little dove."

I whimper. "I know who this pussy belongs to."

He groans and shifts his hand between us to release his cock. "Good fucking girl."

Cain pulls back to position himself and thrusts inside me in one hard stroke.

We both moan with pleasure. He moves hard and fast, pounding me against the truck, his face buried in my neck.

"Fuck," he says against my skin. "If I had fucking lost you..."

"I'm yours." I hold on tighter and dig my nails into his shoulders. "I'm not going anywhere."

The metal of the truck is cold against my ass. We're both covered in blood and dirt. It's not pretty or romantic.

But it's fucking perfect.

"I'm going to fill your pussy, and you're going to feel me inside of you until we stop for the night."

I'm moaning and crying his name, already close to coming from the erratic, uncontrolled way he's fucking me.

"Please," I beg.

"Such a good girl, always so fucking good for me."

His hand slides between us, and his fingers brush along my sensitive clit. "Come for me, little dove."

The command combined with his touch sends me over the edge. I bite down on his shoulder to muffle my cry as I clench around him.

He follows seconds later, and I feel him pulse inside me. The sounds he makes are feral and unhinged. It makes me want to beg him to fuck me all over again.

We stay pressed together against the truck for a few moments, both fighting to breathe.

"We need to keep moving," he says finally. But he isn't letting go of me.

"I know." I cup his face. "Let me wrap those wounds first. It'll take two minutes."

He lowers my feet to the ground, and I pull up my panties and jeans. I grab the first-aid kit from our bags.

The cut on his arm is deep but clean. I work fast and press gauze against it until the bleeding slows, then wrap it. The cut on his ribs is a small slice, so I clean it and place another bandage.

"That'll hold until we can get somewhere safer," I say.

"Get in the truck."

And just like that, we are on the road again.

"Are we still going north?" I ask.

"Yes." He reaches over and rests his hand on my thigh. "I know a place we can cross, and then we'll disappear."

"Won't they keep coming for us?" It seems unrealistic that they would just stop. "Didn't Keegan say something about Dane Sinclair? He's high up in the Ravens."

"I think I know how to handle Dane Sinclair." He glances over at me. "You wanted a beach house, right?"

I laugh. "That was just a silly dream."

We're on the run from some of the most powerful men in the world. I don't think playing house on the beach is in my future.

"If you want it, you are going to fucking have it."

I stare at him in disbelief. "I don't understand why you would do any of this for me. You have known me for all of four days and almost got yourself killed. You can fuck and own any woman you want. Why me?"

He slams on the brakes in the middle of the country road and puts the truck in park. He shifts so that he is completely focused on me.

"Because I fucking love you, little dove."

My mouth drops open. I didn't expect him to actually say the words. "You love me?"

"Yeah. I do." He grips my thigh. "You're mine. I love you. Deal with it."

I unbuckle my seatbelt and crawl into his lap. "I told you that I choose you, asshole. That means I love you, too. Even when you're being a domineering dick about it."

His mouth quirks slightly. "I'm going to make you pay for that. You are going to sob for hours before I allow you to come."

I kiss him hard, then whisper against his lips.

"Pretty fucking please, Cain."

EPILOGUE

CAIN: Three Months Later

The address Dane Sinclair sent is for an abandoned warehouse outside Toronto. Men like us don't do fucking coffee shops.

I glance at Briar in the passenger seat. She's checking her gun for the third time since we left the apartment.

"You could stay in the car."

She looks at me as if I'm an idiot. I'll let that go for now, but she will remember who is in control here.

"We're partners, Cain. And you taught me to shoot and fight so I can handle situations like this. I'm not letting you walk into a trap."

"It's not a fucking trap."

"You don't know that."

I don't. But I'm confident enough in my leverage that Dane won't kill me. At least not until after he gets what he wants.

"If this goes wrong—"

"It won't." She slides the gun into the holster at her hip. "And if it does, I'm a better shot than you think."

That's true. She's a fast learner and has become dangerous with a gun.

I pull into the warehouse parking lot. Dane's black sedan is already there, parked near the entrance. He's leaning against it, arms crossed, looking like he owns the entire city. Which, for all I know, he probably does.

"Stay close to me," I tell Briar as we get out.

"Always."

We approach together. Dane's eyes move from me to Briar. He doesn't appear surprised that I brought her.

"Cain Mercer." He sounds almost amused. "I was starting to think you'd lost your nerve."

"My girl here wanted lunch first. And what my girl wants, my girl gets."

Better he understands that Briar is my motivation here.

Dane pushes off the car. "Let's talk terms then. You accessed your computer two weeks ago. I received your encrypted message. It appears you have something I want, and now I'm here. You've got balls, I'll give you that."

"I protect what's mine."

"We have that in common." Dane's expression doesn't change. "So you found something in Roland Whitmore's files during your mission?"

He glances at Briar again on that last word.

Briar shifts beside me. Her hand rests near her weapon.

"I have everything," I say. "Whitmore's business records. His connections to Gerald Marsh particularly interest you, it would seem. As are his dealings with the Ashworth family. I also have every piece of dirt he collected about council members. All of it."

Dane's jaw tightens.

"Marsh is a fucking problem," Dane says angrily. "He's been operating outside our authority. Skimming from the Ashworth accounts. Making unauthorized moves that could expose the entire organization."

"Sounds like you need proof."

"I need everything you have." Dane takes a step closer. "Every file. Every record. Every connection Roland documented."

"And in exchange? Everything has a price, Sinclair."

He laughs. "What's to stop me from killing you after I have what I want? It would certainly be easier."

"Nothing, I suppose," I say honestly. "But I'm not a bad friend to have if you find you need one."

Dane contemplates what I've said. He knows there are few he can trust, and the information I will hand over to him further confirms that.

"I'll make you officially dead on paper. Both of you." Dane looks at Briar. "The council calls off the hunt. No more running. No more looking over your shoulders. You disappear completely, and the Ravens forget you ever existed. But you stay gone unless I say otherwise."

Briar's hand tightens on my arm.

"And Gerald Marsh?"

"Marsh won't be a problem anymore." Dane's voice is cold. "For anyone."

I consider this. It's a good deal. Better than I expected.

"I want confirmation that we've been announced to the world as dead. I want proof."

"You'll have it within two weeks." Dane pulls out his phone. "Send me the files now. All of them."

I pull out the flash drive I've been carrying.

"This is everything," I hand it to him. "Business records, personal correspondence, financial statements, video surveillance. If it was in Whitmore's files, it's there."

Dane takes it and slides it into his pocket. "Two weeks. I'll contact you with confirmation. After that, you're ghosts."

He turns to leave, then stops.

"One more thing, Mercer. Don't make me regret this. If you resurface, if you cause problems, if you give me any reason to think you're a liability—"

"We won't."

"Good." Dane gets into his car. "Well played, Mercer. Enjoy your freedom."

We watch him drive away. The warehouse parking lot is silent except for the sound of Briar's breathing beside me.

We're actually free.

"Cain—" Briar starts, but I'm already pulling her toward our car.

The second we're inside, I kiss her. My hand wraps around the back of her neck.

"We're free," I say against her mouth. "Do you understand? We're actually fucking free."

She laughs and presses her forehead to mine. "I can't believe that just worked."

"I told you it would work."

"You said you were confident. That's not the same thing." She climbs over the center console and straddles my lap. "But you were right."

Her hands are already working on my belt. And I grab her throat so that I can kiss her.

There's nothing gentle about this. I don't do gentle. I need to feel my girl after months of running.

I shove her jeans and panties down her hips, and then awkwardly pull them from her body.

She positions herself back on top of me, rubbing her wet pussy along my cock.

“Fuck.”

“Remember the first time I straddled you like this? And now look at us.”

She raises up higher so I can enter her, but she knows I won’t let her set the pace. I grip her hips and pull her down onto my cock as I thrust up into her.

“That’s it,” I growl. “I needed you.”

She rides me with her head thrown back, gasping. But I’m the one in control. I’m always in control with her.

When she comes, she buries her face against my neck to muffle her scream. I follow seconds later, holding her tight against me as I release deep inside of her.

She's mine. Always mine.

We stay like that for a few minutes. Breathing hard.

She’s still in my lap with my cock still inside her, and I reach into the backseat and pull out a folder I’ve been keeping hidden.

“What’s that?” Briar asks.

I hand it to her. “Open it.”

She does. Inside are printouts of beach houses. Five different properties in three different countries.

"You've been looking at houses?"

"I promised you a beach house." I brush her hair back from her face. "Pick one, little dove. Anywhere you want. We'll start our new lives there."

"Do I have to take a new name?"

"To everyone else, we'll be whoever we need to be." I cup her face. "But to me you'll always be Briar Ashley Mercer. That's your name. You're fucking mine forever."

"Can we actually get married? Legally, I mean?"

"You want to be my wife, little dove? Then you're my fucking wife. Right here, right now. No church, no paperwork, just you and me. Are you mine, little dove?"

"Of course." She presses her forehead to mine. "Are you mine?"

"Fucking always." I wrap my arms tighter around her.

She kisses me.

"I love you," she whispers against my mouth.

"I know." I pull her closer. "And I fucking love you too."

She laughs and smacks my chest. "Asshole."

"Your asshole husband now." I lift her off of me and set her in her seat so she can get her jeans on. "Now pick a house. I need to know where I'm taking us."

I don't give a fuck where it is.

I lay my hand on her thigh.

There's only one thing I need.

And she's fucking mine.

****

Want a little more Cain and Briar?

I have a treat for you! Join my mailing list for an additional super spicy scene and a look at Cain and Briar's new life. Get your copy here: https://dl.bookfunnel.com/kx6m0431d9

Want more Ravens?

Pre-order the newest book in my world now, Devour! (Dane and Whitney will be there, too!) https://dahliavale.com/devour/

Want the inside scoop on my Ravens world? How about an exclusive Sinclair serial that keeps the Sinclairs story going? Join my patreon! There's even a free tier! https://www.patreon.com/cw/dahliavale

You don't want to miss the Sinclair men!

STALK ME, PLEASE!

Here are all kinds of ways that you can stalk me and I'd love to have you!

Website: https://dahliavale.com/

Mailing list: Join my mailing list to stay informed on freebies, upcoming releases, promotions, character art reveals and so much more!

Patreon: https://www.patreon.com/cw/dahliavale

Discord: https://discord.com/invite/TztNw94Uv7

Facebook Group: https://www.facebook.com/groups/dahliaslittledoves

Instagram: https://www.instagram.com/dahliavaleauthor

TikTok: https://www.tiktok.com/@dahliavaleauthor

Shop: https://shop.dahliavale.com/

Join My Groups

Want to keep in touch? Be sure to join in on my various reader groups where you can chat all things The Ravens and dark romance reads! I'd love to be able to connect personally with you!

Facebook Group: https://www.facebook.com/groups/dahliaslittledoves

Discord: https://discord.gg/EqDyxTgc

Patreon: https://www.patreon.com/cw/DahliaVale(This is where you will also find the Patreon-exclusive Sinclair serial!)

Character Art

Join my mailing list today to get access to character art for Stolen Dove and other books as they are commissioned! https://subscribepage.io/dvcharacters

Dahlia's Books

My entire world connects through *The Ravens*, with just enough crossover to make every story a little more dangerous, and a lot more fun.

For my most up-to-date book list, visit: dahliavale.com

Standalones:

- Stolen Dove

The Sinclairs: Where redemption costs everything—and love is the deadliest game of all.

The Sinclairs have everything—money, influence, and a name that commands fear. But beneath their polished empire lies *The Ravens*, a secret society built on control, corruption, and legacy oaths sealed in blood. Dane, Fox, Tate, and Thorne were born to dominate. To protect their legacy. To never fall in lov e.Until love becomes the one thing that might destroy them. In a world of forbidden desire and dangerous power, their women become both their weakness... and their salvation.

- Fallen Dane
- Savage Fox
- Twisted Tate
- Broken Thorne

The Ravens:

- Devour

Appreciation

There are so many incredible people—both new and longtime ride-or-dies—who have supported me on this wild writing journey. Authors, readers, friends, family, co-workers... you know who you are. I'd list every one of you if I had a few extra pages (and a really small font). Just know this: I adore you, and I'm endlessly grateful.

Steve: My husband, tech wizard, idea bouncer, chef, laundry hero, and all-around MVP. You believe in my big, bold dreams even when they sound like total chaos. Thank you for being my partner in every possible way. Love you, babe.

Dexter and Felix: My boys, my chaos gremlins, and the source of many laughs. You're excellent at distracting me mid-sentence, but you're also the inspiration behind some of the snarky sibling banter that sneaks into my books. One day you'll realize your mom writes smut... and I'll probably owe you both ice cream and therapy. Love you forever.

Rachel, Nina & Brittany: My mom, aunt, and sister—aka my built-in cheer squad. You've supported me through every high, low, and harebrained idea I've ever chased. You hold all my most embarrassing stories, so let's make sure you never talk to anyone without legal counsel present. I love you all dearly.

Erin: From the moment fate brought us together in the most unexpected way, we knew we were meant to be besties. Thank you for listening to every rant, dream, plot twist in life, and meltdown—and for always helping me find my way back to joy and clarity. You're pure magic.

Courtney: Fate handed me a twin flame in the author world. We literally finish each other's sentences (or just say the same thing) and have become legit besties. I can't wait for the day we meet in person.

Thank you for our pretty much all day, every day chats, late-night idea storms, the pep talks, and all the chaos we've embraced together. We've got this, twinsie!

Bliss: Who knew a smutty follow train on Insta would bring me one of my dearest friendsies? Thank you for the endless texts, laughter, spicy scene brainstorming, feedback on my chaos, and all-around moral support. So lucky we found each other!

To my **ARC and Street Team**: Your love, feedback, and support make my heart full. Thank you for shouting about these stories from the rooftops—you make this adventure feel like a party I never want to leave.

And to all the amazing **author friends** and **influencers** I've met through social media: You're one of the best, most unexpected blessings of this entire journey. Thank you for the inspiration, the laughs, the advice—and most of all, for welcoming me into this magical community.

Meet the Leading Dove

Dahlia Vale is a bestselling author of unapologetically dark, fast-paced, and deliciously unhinged romance. Her stories are filled with dangerous men, defiant women, and the kind of heat that could burn down an empire.

When she's not crafting worlds ruled by secret societies and morally gray alphas, Dahlia can usually be found in Northern Maine, juggling caffeine, chaos, and her two boys, along with her husband and Kindle never far away.

She's obsessed with horror movies, Bridgerton, Jessica Rabbit, Michael Myers, Chucky dolls, the Grinch, listening to nothing but the *Hamilton* soundtrack, and anything pink.

Dahlia also writes steamy Regency romance as **Christina Diane**—perfect for the fellow Bridgerton lovers out there!

She loves connecting with readers and swapping dark book recs! Visit dahliavale.com or find her on social media—she'd love to hear from you.

www.ingramcontent.com/pod-product-compliance
Lightning Source LLC
LaVergne TN
LVHW090951080826
845145LV00003B/968

* 9 7 8 1 9 6 4 7 1 3 4 5 8 *